FROG GIG AND OTHER STORIES

FROG GIG AND
OTHER STORIES

BY SPEER MORGAN

A *Breakthrough Book*
University of Missouri Press, 1976
Columbia & London

"The Oklahoma and Western" first appeared in *Atlantic Monthly*, November 1974.

"The Bad Cat" first appeared in *Fiction Midwest* (*Tales*), October 1973.

"Momma and the Moonman" first appeared in *Northwest Review* 14, no. 2.

"Frog Gig" first appeared in *Place* 2, no. 1.

"The Bullet" first appeared in *The Iowa Review* 4. Outlaw details and documents from Glenn Shirley, *Law West of Fort Smith* (Bison Book Edition, 1968).

University of Missouri, Columbia, Missouri 65201

Library of Congress Catalog Card Number 76–22791

Printed and bound in the United States of America

Library of Congress Cataloging in Publication Data

Morgan, Speer, 1949–
  Frog Gig, and other stories.

  (A Breakthrough book)
  I. Title.
PZ4.M85137Fr   [PS3563.087149]   813'.5'4   76–22791
ISBN 0–8262–0206–3

This book is published with the assistance of an award from the American Council of Learned Societies.

FOR EARLINE MCBEATH

CONTENTS

FROG GIG AND OTHER STORIES

1

THE OKLAHOMA
AND WESTERN

YOU can't get visible in New York, and San Francisco just doesn't cut it any more, so you serve time in this junkyard. I live here now so I won't have to in the future. At first you think Jesus, what a circus. Walking to the studio on Sunset Boulevard, doorways mutter to you, "Hey man, I can fix your mouth, your nose, your arm. . . ." Hands reach out and grab you. "Give me five bucks, daddy. My old lady needs a glass eye." A fifteen year old walks by in drag with the latest hairstyle—burned down to his scalp. At the corner a pale man with sloping shoulders gives you a manifesto: "The Right to Be Dying Humans." You pass signs: Institute of Oral Sex / Sheer Erotic Education / Degrees Given. Across the street: Wrestle Nude Women / The Real Thing. As you approach the studio, sirens begin to wail across the city. It's summer, no rain, and each day the sun rises to poison. It's setting now somewhere over the ocean, the gauzy-whitened eye of a dead fish.

But you get used to it. You join the sideshow. The other day in the supermarket, my own little girl started a big fight with me. In this place they open meat, bread, pickles, mustard, and make sandwiches right in the stores. A guy with a poor boy was watching us. The argument was nothing new—we'd been having it off and on for weeks—but it was a new twist, because this time Katie had decided to resolve it by exposing me to the public. She got that damn squinched-up look on her face and said, "Daddy, you smoke narcotics. I've told you it's bad for you, and now I'm going to tell everybody in the store." She immediately started pulling people on the arm, saying, "That man over there, my daddy, smokes narcotics. That man over there, my daddy, smokes narcotics," which aroused only minimal interest from anybody except the guy with the sandwich, who had hair down to his elbows and a luminous glaze in his eye. He came over to me and said, "Hey brother, haven't you found Jesus yet? You'll never OD on him." And I had to stand in front of the meat counter arguing with him that I don't smoke marijuana, dammit; it's bad for my ambition; I just smoke tobacco, and I can't help it if Jesus wouldn't like that either.

I was telling him the truth. I smoke nothing but air and Tareytons now. Pharmaceuticals and coke, of course, people are always giving them to me. I seldom buy the stuff. If you've got talent and something going, they'll feed it to you like a queen bee. At the big parties, it's kind of a thing, you know, when somebody takes you off into a bedroom and says, "Shut the door." *Snuff, snuff.* "You know Freud did it for seven years," somebody always says, "and Hitler . . . a-a-achoo!" Before the circle breaks, you'll all be standing there with that metal taste down to your stomach and a kind of pleasant new freeway with no cars on it, leading from your sinuses up through two hundred miles of brain out the top of your skull, and energy pouring down your throat, down your shoulders and arms like ice water, and maybe for just a second you glance around at each other and there's a brotherhood, a softness anyway, before you all grow back your alligator hides and rattlesnake neckties.

I got started in music up in San Francisco in the good old days. I was up there for three years trying to make a band out of a bunch of bums. Then I wrote some stuff for a famous group up in Mendocino—famous on one song—but they were already losing it, acting senile except for maybe five minutes a day when all their chemicals flowed smoothly together. Now they're all dead, divorced, burned out, and sued. They had one song, just one, that was beautiful, and when I catch myself singing it my hands start to sweat. Back when I wrote for them, they drank pure carrot juice for breakfast, made from Scandanavian carrots in a twelve hundred dollar juicer, and then began a rigorous day of fifteen to twenty joints apiece, all pre-rolled in a silver king-size cigar box with a cameo of Batista on the lid, all the white stuff they could find and assorted pills to take the edge from Ups, give the Downs a little gusto and invest the Just Rights with full-bodied pleasure. All in all, it was a relaxing kind of San Francisco suicide, performed among the finest recording and speaker equipment available, turned up so loud that the ranch house and the green hill itself shook. I'd give them a song; they'd get it down after a few tries and then listen quietly to the tape; their heads all bowed in priestly contemplation, while the speakers battered us like an aspirin commercial.

*   *   *

I went to work for a rock-and-roll magazine in San Francisco writing reviews—I'm literate, too, or at least used to be—but most of the people I knew then have since been fired or quit. That magazine is a tomb with a bunch of good-looking, ambitious mummies walking around in it. The offices are like going back to your hometown grade school after fifteen years of growing up. Yes sir, real exciting there at the journalistic heart of R & R—lots of sound, fury, smoke, dope, deals, and wheels—the Wizard of Oz behind his little curtain operating the boom-boom gadgets. There's one guy now who keeps the place from falling apart, and he's got a cork up his ass like a Wall Street accountant. He's mildly dudish, leathery rich hip; he tells jokes like he never expects people to laugh at them, and he's as dependable as a cow. He clunks around the offices in expensive boots, eyeing people like a Presbyterian minister in a home for unwed mothers, keeping it together, keeping psychosis below organization level, and meeting stomach-grinding deadlines, dishing out the hippest sludge in the business with excruciating regularity. A decent straw boss, but a lousy job of work.

San Francisco would not do, so I did gather my household to-gether and moved southward to the Pit, where the winds blow shrouds of desert sand and internal combustion over our house, covering everything, sifting through the windows and dusting even the keys of my closed piano. From this place thirty miles in every direction but the sea, houses elbow each other for room, muttering to themselves, gossipless, and there is no rain to wash the soot from their itching skins or the shit from their yards. When I work at night in this living room, my possum, pet from back home, stays up with me. He appears in one corner, then another, staring clear rings through the room. I got him on a visit back home last summer. He has a pink nose, an ugly dead-skin tail that he drags behind him, and very dark eyes, and sometimes when I'm working late at night he winks at me. Katie gets up in the middle of some nights. Not that the noise bothers her; she could sleep with a guitar plugged in her ear. She just enjoys the company of Possum and me, busy at our appointed labors. Sometimes she holds the animal down for staring contests. She puts her nose right up to his and tells him how much he stinks. And she hassles me about Hollywood, how she wants to be an actress and all. She claims that all her friends are famous but she. I tell her all in due time, but of course that just irritates her.

We're from Oklahoma. There's railroad blood in us. My grandfather, who mostly raised me, was a mechanic for the railroad for forty-one years, and his father was cut into three pieces by a night train outside Atoka, before Indian Territory had become Oklahoma. I have a tintype miniature of Great-Grandfather, taken when he was a young man: his eyes unambiguous and clear as murder, a practical-joker's half smile curled against his face. In the early days he made big money near Whitefield cutting black walnut for gunstocks and furniture, and when the trees ran out he went to work for the railroads, which had been spreading for years across the territory of the Five Civilized Tribes in official reparation for their part in the Civil War. Great-Grandfather was a crew boss to start with and soon higher. He had a good job and family. Then one night in 1893 he got drunk and walked six or seven miles down a spur line with a coal-oil signal lamp, and for no reason anybody could figure, stood in the track and tried to stop a train—in country,

Grandfather used to say, where you flat didn't interfere with an engine unless you had something pretty big to do it with.

Ghostly rail, jack me up and feather me down, make me rich and famous so I can leave this Pit. Rich and famous—and I really will be. Does that tick you off? Kind of like the other side of Lennon's primal scream, ain't it? *I don't believe in Beatles.* That was more outrageous than all the rest. Only I haven't made it yet. Not quite. I'm on the way though and not even scared any more. The crossties are laid, the rails in place. Sometimes I sit up like this and waste time making lists, writing notes and strategies and titles to hits. A good title is half the trip, as you know, like the name of a group: "The Ozark Mountain Daredevils." Those guys have got it made with that name. They could beat on a washtub and sell records. I write eighty to one hundred titles in a night, smoke forty cigarettes, and love myself to death. I mess with my guitar, and sometimes, a good many times, I light up and howl. Kris and Katie are used to it. They could sleep through a Stones concert. The possum slopes around and keeps me company through the night, and we get along just fine. I bought him for $3.50 from a shy Choctaw kid at a filling station not far from Atoka.

Possums aren't too smart, but they have good instincts. Once some big people were over here listening to new stuff, and he crawled up the side of the chair and sat on my shoulder while I sang. His claws were like razors, but I didn't let on, because I knew that sight was better than a full-length hype on my fascinating Okie background. A coarse ball of bristly fur on four delicate pink feet that each walk separately and with creepy smoothness, as if out of some night forest where children walk in dreams, and those sloe depthless eyes looking at nothing in particular—a galvanic image, if I do say so myself—perched there on my shoulder, as I plucked and sang for the hotshots.

People have tried to call me "Possum," but I won't let them— too familiar. You've got to pick up every stitch.

I used to be a thief: drove all over eastern Oklahoma in my '55

Ford, singing along with WNOE, and stealing money out of pop boxes outside filling stations and stores. By myself with a decent set of keys, I made fifty bucks every working night. I was a hood, I guess. I bit a guy's ear off once, which is another thing they like to hear about out here. I told that story to the president of a record company once, and he offered me my first contract. That was in New York. I had sent him a tape, and he called back and asked me to come up. "I like the cuts," he said. "Fantastic lyrics, but you're going to need good production. And I want to see if you have charisma." I was asleep, kind of—he had awakened me with the call—and I said, "You don't have to fly me to New York to find that out. I can tell you over the phone. I have charisma. I got it out my ass." He flew me up anyway, and somehow we got around to biting the guy's ear off back in Oklahoma, and that was when he offered me the contract. This wasn't any cheese-faced promo man but the president of what was then the biggest label in the business. I told him maybe. Everybody back here said I was out of my mind, that I should suck up that contract like a Popsickle. But I was lucky I didn't. He got fired six months later over a payola scandal, and I ended up with a better contract here.

My label is the biggest in R & R now. The president is twenty-nine years old, and he's made a million dollars for every one of them. He's a criminal, but I kind of like him. He likes me okay, too, but if he didn't think I'd make him some money, he'd have his secretary cut my nuts off. I went to see him a year ago to talk about an advance, a modest $4,300 to be exact, and he said, "Goddammit, people are always asking me for money. You people think I'm a vending machine of some kind? Write him a check, Jane. How much did you say?" I told him I didn't want a single stinking cent of his money and started to walk out, but he leaned over his desk and said, "Yes, you do. You want it now," and he pounded his desk (*thunk*) "and you'll want it again," (*thunk*) "and again, and again," (*thunk*) "*and again!*"

He was right. Sometimes he can be real friendly. He once told me the key to our relationship. We were at a topless organic bar,

6

where executives go to drink apple juice and make fun of tits. "Look," he said, "there's one thing you have to do for me. Just one thing. You have to make yourself indispensable. You can cuss me; you can make outrageous demands; you can fool with my secretary; and as long as I need you enough, I'll take it. That's it, baby."

He works twenty hours a day, makes an endless number of telephone calls—a hundred thousand words—every one of them designed to make money. He pays $160 a week to talk to a psychiatrist, and he uses no drugs except prescribed downers to get to sleep. When they ran low on record vinyl because of the oil embargo, he fired almost half of the nontechnical employees and every unestablished artist in the company except me. I'm the only gamble on the label now. Before that, he held my first record up for fifteen months, and I learned pretty quickly that the key isn't exactly what he said. The key is to make the demands and cuss him now if I have to, to show him every way he looks that I could give a damn whether he keeps me or not and with all the slouch I can muster. It takes a painted face to attract that bastard and keep his attention, because he lives somewhere out there in a pure blizzard of money. Reaching him takes everything you've got and just a little bit more. You have to tickle, move and surprise him, amaze him with your crudeness, wit, subtlety. And when he talks back you listen carefully, because a machine in the back of his head is arranging those words to conjure the maximum amount of dollars. You can always trust him if you know that.

It's not I who makes me indispensable, but his idea of me. He didn't spend a red cent promoting my first album—no telephone calls, no tour, no gimmicks, no coke to the big stations. He just put the album on the market and waited for it to sink. But I've got friends and a telephone myself. The reviews were decent but not hot. They were mostly impressed by my backup people—one of Lennon's old drummers, two of the biggest women in town, and a bunch of others who wouldn't even take money for helping me—most of them—because they could have wiped their feet on me and they knew it. They like me.

7

Because I'm pretty elegant as Okie stars go: I have a possum, a wife with Indian blood and a mind like a giant Wurlitzer jukebox with water bubbling up the sides in five colors, a whole show to fill the room with sound and light. I can make your pulse rise. Imitations? I sing early Dylan better than Dylan. I can sound like guitars, drums, and horns with just my mouth. The musicians love that most of all, because in the studio I can show them a song part fast. I can make your favorite singer, the one with the full crystal voice, sing for me alone and desire me for a closer friend. Not that she's eyed me that way quite yet, but when she does I'll just have to make her desire me more. After all, I'm a married man with an eleven-year-old kid. I'll sing, I'll snort, I'll swim in the nude with her, but I won't get close enough to let her hate me. Business aside, I wouldn't want that to happen anyway. She's nice. At the studio she sometimes works with all the lights out and just a candle on her piano. She does cast that spell of sorrow and lost innocence. She's not engineered. And she's a regular cannibal at business. She learned a long time ago that in this place you're either a mere head or a hunter, and the mere heads lose every way. She drives her own Rolls; no chauffer.

I still drive a Dodge Dart, which makes me kind of quaint around here, but then again that's why they still love me, because I'm a down-home boy who's got it but ain't made it yet. After you're up there, they suck your blood and wait for you to make mistakes or to kill yourself like most of the really big ones who don't turn into zombies at thirty-five—like Dylan if he hadn't broken his neck and walked out of the hospital believing in the Old Testament.

When were we innocent? In the sixties? Back in the holy days when the best group in San Francisco made it without one single hit? When they hung out on their farm smoking dope grown specially for them by a contractor in Mexico, obeying their leader like Stalin, shooting their thirty-aught-sixes and automatic pistols for entertainment, and giving that endless train of sweethearts a free ride on the roller coaster of quick fame? Or Janis Joplin, who never claimed to be looking for anything but the ultimate spasm,

8

hurting for her audiences like someone much older, her mind a bed of snakes and her life a mess to obliterate, singing her throat raw, boogying loose at full tilt for a hit sweeter than the needle? Or Jimi Hendrix dominating his guitar at Monterey Pop with "Wild Thing," playing it upside down and backwards, as if there was something just ever so nicely obscene about the way he used his instrument to death—tamed, broke, pissed on it with lighter fluid and brought it to flames—the band still going behind him as he hunched and sneered over its destruction and yet still loved it, feedback from the flames growling, barking through the speakers like a live thing in agony and then falling to silence, ending the song in ashes, wistful disgust.

Innocent? Was I innocent driving my '55 Ford through the hills of eastern Oklahoma singing along with WNOE and looking for pop boxes to break into? I guess I wasn't. When you get married at sixteen and have a kid a month later, it's hard to stay innocent. I wasn't just a juvenile delinquent but a married man, a thief, and I was lucky I didn't get sent to McAlester. But that's a whole different story. Kris is a quarter Cherokee, and she hung in there pretty tough. We smashed lamps on the floor, knocked holes in walls, and chased each other around with knives. One time we were driving somewhere, and she kicked me in the leg so hard that I had to stop the car. I tried to strangle her, and would have done it too, if a blood vein hadn't burst like red lightning across her eye at the same instant she cracked me breathless in the ribs. More than once, I hated Kris enough to dream of poison, and I could hate little Katie just as much. Alone with her, I would sometimes let her squawl in dirty diapers to get back at her for being born. I would squawl back, mocking her in the futile wish that she could feel my spite. I was a bad father. I still am. Very unprofessional. But she's alive, as pretty as her momma and twice as mean, going to a fancy Hollywood school, and our family will stay together unless one of us dies. Even back then, I knew we had to stay together no matter what, no matter if our duplex became a prison of outrage. And I drove away from that house every night through the quiet hills in my skin of steel, dreaming of fortune in the light of my radio, learning to sing with Elvis and Fats and a dozen others whom I remember to this moment better than any house or room.

Katie is eleven now and we're only twenty-seven, which will be nice in a few years. You've got to be ignorant to have kids, just like you've got to be ignorant to get married or be a star. If you understand all the implications of it, you'll never do it. I have friends now approaching thirty who still don't have a kid, and their ideas about families are getting more and more complicated. By the time they have one, their heads will be worn out and grey worrying about it. The first step is ignorance; ambition itself is ignorance, and without it nothing gets done.

Kris and I get along better now. She's into speed a little bit and pretty well off my back about L.A. Speed is her trip—strictly pharmaceutical, though—none of that homemade crap, and with a time-release downer that makes eight hours as smooth as glass. She never takes more than one at a time. Bad? Hell yes, it's bad. They even made a bad movie about it a few years ago. It can kill you. But L.A. will kill you faster, and we're in a race to beat it. I take a lot of stuff myself, like I said before, but once I get out of here with a reputation and buy some land back east, I'll be independent of the scene, the ten thousand bloodsuckers and their drugs, and able to work at sessions in Nashville or anywhere. That sounds idealistic, doesn't it, but watch me.

I spend hours making calls and waiting for people, just waiting for technicians, promo men, musicians, everybody, to make up their minds about things. With a lot of them you learn to act totally insane. It's the only way to get their attention. You exaggerate, you call them names, "You *stupid* son of a bitch, that's *not* what I want." You'd be surprised at how often that works. If you're not ready, though, I mean on top of the situation, they'll hype you out the door. How do you get ready day after scorching, rainless, smog-itching day? You take what you have to, you paw and snort, you put on your crazy face, and come at the bastards like Attila the Hun.

Maybe that's just my way of doing it. But that's what we're

here for, isn't it? Here in this midnight ball on the San Andreas Fault, where we work in masquerade in windowless studios, passing around a prophylactic heavy as a cow's udder—part of someone's tax return converted to powder—breathing it for thirty-six hours until our nerves are white and brittle, and we are working like blind masters to get down harmonies that will make you feel so good; in this Fat Tuesday where leather coats, hands covered with jade rings, pants stitched by psychotic fags with heavy reputations, blouses clinging wetly to prodigal skin, where English cars guaranteed for life, cedar sauna baths, and all the rest stand perfected in George Washington's shrewd gaze, saying yes we're making it, motherfucker, but watch out, we're outlaws, savages, we're ugly or too beautiful to care, we can't be trusted, our faces are cut free, our moves agile as silver-eyed wolves, and if we suffer it's from too much of every wish.

And can you lose it in the factory of dreams? I worry about that sometimes. But no, I'm not. I'm up and coming in the year of our Lord 1974, and when you hear my music you'll love what you think I am. You and the teenies both, because not even a genius can get off the ground now without the teenies and their billion-dollar hunger for hits under three minutes with good titles and catchy choruses. But you too will love me, because I'm already smuggling art across in my lyrics, producing to hit but writing to last.

Kris is my best ear. I sing and watch her face. She always says it's good, fantastic; but I can tell by her expression when it's really money sound, especially those Cherokee eyes, which never lie unless she's peaking out on something, at which times she likes everything—my songs, the sound of the washing machine, a pallid sunset against the kitchen window. . . . Me, I like less and less out there, the ten thousand bloodsuckers and their impediments one after another, and I'm learning to cut through them like butter.

Last year I went to a lot of Hollywood parties and hung around with stars. I even went to see a Beatle once. He was slouched down in a lounge chair almost horizontally and had a tired look on his face. When I was introduced, he waved bleakly and murmured, "Aello. I'm a Bea-le." I was walking the ceiling on a couple of weeks of speed and talked a lot. I got worked up telling him my theory about "A Hard Day's Night," a real theoretical oration that must have lasted twenty to twenty-five minutes, criticism as well as praise. He just sat there, looking at me steadily with a weak smile, occasionally agreeing. When I finally got through, he said with surprising vigor, but somehow like a college professor feigning interest in a book report, "I want you to know that I quite agree with what you've said. Quite agree." Then he slid from his chair, levitated himself, hobbled across the room like his legs were asleep, bumped into a glass table, turned profile to me and said thoughtfully, still in a friendly tone, but vaguely troubled, "Kind of like the Jap stock market . . . ain't we? . . ."

Then there was the time the famous sex starlet patted me on the privates. My former manager took me over to visit her. He's only a couple of years older than I, went to Harvard, writes western and horror movies, and talks constantly about sex. He insisted that I take my possum. He acted like we were going to some kind of private showing, which in a way it turned out to be. At the front door, she was raw to the waist, wearing a bikini bottom, and nursing a baby. She said, "Hi, this is Baby, maybe God, we're not sure yet." So I introduced my possum as Possum, maybe Elephant, he ain't fully grown yet. Ho-ho. Ahem. Her nose was red, and she had the sniffles from doing coke. It was in a Chinese sugar bowl on the living-room table, along with a couple of rolled, pinned bills to snort it through, a one and a hundred. She explained that the sugar bowl had come from one of Chairman Mao's factories, and she offered us some coke. It was sweet, without too much speed; the kind that lays you back for a while before the edge comes on. She put the top back on the sugar bowl and nursed her baby. I told her I hoped Baby made it to God, but wouldn't it be kind of strange when she got older and you were sitting at dinner. Pass the green beans, please God. Or when she got to be a teenager, and you made her do the chores. Take the garbage out, God. She sniffled and smiled at me across space, like I had just spoken a sublime mantra. Her face reminded me of 1968, San Francisco, only rich and famous, and Baby suckled her most noisily.

I sat for a while trying to think of something to talk about besides the possum, which was hard to do with all this maternal ecstasy filling the room, here on the very bosom that the workers of America, the tired and weary workers, the impatient teenagers, and yes, even the frustrated executives and their pickled wives have spent millions to see on the screen. I told her that back where I came from, people in the hills still thought there was something evil about possums, being ratty looking and nocturnal and all, and there was a superstition that the male possum had a forked penis that he stuck into the female's nose to inseminate her. Her eyes got real big and interested, so I talked on about the possum's thirteen-day gestation period, the shortest of any mammal, and how the infants crawl out of the uterus on their own, hardly more than worms of scum but with good front claws to hang onto momma's nipples—thirteen nipples, twelve in a horseshoe shape with one in the middle—safe there in the pouch until they grow into strong little possums. She didn't believe me, and I explained that possums were related to kangaroos—they were both marsupials, the lowest form of mammal. She was still incredulous. Finally she gave me her baby to hold and got out an encyclopedia to look it up. It impressed the hell out of her when she discovered that it was true. She sat down beside me on the couch, her face strangely lit up and glowing. "That's *really* amazing. The *lowest* form!"

I was getting nervous. She's a blonde, so unlike Kris, and you know how that can be. She leaned over and played with Baby in my lap without taking her back, and I really started getting uptight. My manager leered at us from across the room, and Possum had ceased exploring the rug and wandered beneath a chair. His scaly tail stuck out. I could smell the milk on her breasts as she leaned over me—the kind of odor, I must admit, that could make an old rock-and-roll rooster clear his throat and cockadoodledoo once more. Pretty soon, it seemed like I had to keep that baby over my lap. Of course, then she took her back, and I lost it entirely, went hot in the face, and stared down like a true Okie with my mouth open at my pants, which were standing up like the Washington Monument. I said something stupid, an attempted joke that I have since forgotten. Then she did it. She reached down, patted my pants gently three times, and said, "That's okay. It's organic."

When we left the house, my manager split into a grin. "Need some crutches?" I told him to shut up. In his Porsche he choked out laughing, glancing at me back and forth like he always does. "You know the word on her. Her own agent's been talking all over town that she's had it. Sixty thousand dollars on coke last year, and five or six visits to the cracker box. She blew a bunch of tests. . . ." We whined down through the hills in second gear, and I drifted away from what else he said. Railed to the ears, I was weirded out, because the actress had not been kidding, not Mae Westing me, but stupidly serious with her assurance and vague smile, distant in all her famous flesh and snowy as the ghost on a busted TV.

The energy in me was bitter. Business flashed into my mind, and I had the not unusual urge to go somewhere and eat the blood-suckers alive, pull them apart with my teeth if necessary, to get them moving on my record, which had then been rusting for nine months. But my stomach heaved with thick automatic laughter, like drunkard's vomit, and in a funny way I didn't give a damn. Possum blinked once slowly, putting his claws through my shirt to grasp on through the curves, and I held him against me.

*   *   *

I don't cultivate stars any more. I won't even go to a Dylan party. I've missed two of those, and five years ago I would have stood myself up against a wall and riddled myself with hot slugs for missing a chance to observe Dylan get into a taxi at fifty yards. I know something now. I'm smarter than Dylan, can sing better, and write better lyrics. Ain't that the shits. So I have to keep it together. The burden of genius, you know—it's hard on your nerves. I stay home at night working, watching these earthquake-cracked walls, and Possum sniffing through the rooms on his silent, businesslike rounds. I've written three songs in the last week, and one of them is very good, I'd almost say classic. The company has an acetate with ten cuts on it, including six potential singles. It's in New York now. They have to agree with L.A. on what to make a hit out of, because nowadays it takes even more money and favors from both coasts to get a single out there, and without a single, no album sales, etc., etc. For a while people believed in music enough to advertise it by word of mouth, and the new FM stations played whole albums and shucked the cream puff entirely. That sold good music. Now FM is back to commercial, mostly canned, tapes complete with DJs and music from L.A., New York, Philadelphia. But I don't care, I'm making my music, it's good and getting better, and not long from now I'll be off the ground. The vampires are moving faster for me now.

I usually go to bed before sunrise so I don't have to see it, but yesterday Katie got up early and came in while I was still working. "Dad-dey," she whined like a sleepy baby and grabbed onto my arm. I sang her a new song about railroads, the railroad blood in our own past, the continental line that tied this country together and webbed it with steel, and her great-great-grandfather drunk one night and cut to pieces on a spur of the Oklahoma and Western. I sang of him walking through the cool night and counting oak rails for miles, lost to who knows what purpose, like a boy at play, behind a face, though, that could never look boyish, but, like any man's face eighty years ago, was bitten by need, and drunk, as he dangled the signal lantern down the track; I sang of the mystery of him standing his ground and swaying the lantern in a ruby arc for the pot-bellied iron he must have known wouldn't stop, and the dim white eye bearing down on him in a fury of steam. I sang it to her in that moment before day when the nighttime has dried, and she rubbed her eyes and listened to some of it before going into the bathroom. I went to the door and sang the rest to her, and when she finally came back out, she was awake and acting haughty. I asked her how she liked it.

Instead of answering, she said, "I want to make ads. All the other kids at school get to. There's a stupid boy in the *fourth* grade who makes them for Nabisco. Every time I look, *he's* on TV. Will you get me a good agent?"

"Agent? What do you want to sell—gasoline? Foundation garments? You don't even have your breasts yet. You can't get an agent till you have them."

"No, silly. Shampoo or something. Maybe Pepsi. I'm better looking than that boy for sure. Get me an agent."

Muttering, I wandered back into the living room, where day now threatened through the curtains. "You're catching on, baby." I played a few chords of "Oklahoma and Western," but my guitar had gone to sleep in my hands.

2

THE BAD CAT

LATE in the afternoon of her seventy-first birthday Dr. La-
Verne Sparks looked out her kitchen window and, seeing movement behind the snow-covered woodpile in her backyard, put down
a marker that she had been using to label tin cans full of oddments
and went to the utility closet. There she unwrapped the Winchester
carbine her father had taught her to shoot in 1914. From an oily
box kept since her father's death, she extracted three shiny bullets
and loaded the rifle, not at the moment remembering that they were
new, purchased six weeks before and transferred into the box, but
feeling them as his bullets—the single carton he had left when he
died. She felt his presence strongly as she cocked the gun, remembering the smell of dirt, tobacco, and sweat on him as he stood beside
her and with grinding impatience demonstrated how to load and
shoot the rifle. When she finally hit the tin can she did not understand why he knelt, took painful hold of her shoulder and said, "We
will have to provide." And she did not yet understand that the
wildness in his face had come from the doctor who had just visited
and had given Solomon Sparks the first and last physical examination of his life. She thought only of escaping his grasp and the expression in his face, not her father's but some crazy man's, some
Methodist's at an outdoor meeting staring dizzy rings at her, saying, "You will not forget. You will not. There are no sons," then
walking away from her and standing at the edge of the newly plowed
field as if he had suddenly forgotten what he was doing.

She did not remember that they were new bullets, which had
cost her more than a week of embarrassment, carrying the old rifle

in a cloth wrapper around the city—so changed since her retirement from the university that several times she got lost and was forced to ask gas-station attendants to call cabs for her. Once she forgot her address and entirely lost her composure. If her younger sister discovered that LaVerne was wandering the streets carrying an old rifle, she would take her without further ado to St. Louis. She was just waiting for an excuse. And so before her final expedition for bullets, in case she should again forget herself, LaVerne taped a label to her wrist that said Call Cab, 911 Bright Street. Clerks were suspicious when she unwrapped the rifle and asked for shells to fit it. They referred her to worried-looking managers who denied having such shells and recommended other stores, the names of which she printed in the bold rectilinear script she had struck across blackboards for forty-five years in the school of agriculture. She was proud of the script. It still came easily.

Although at times her memory was vivid and insistent, spreading beyond a corner of her mind into her eyes and fingertips, it was no longer reliable. At good moments she knew this, and so with the script cared for herself, labeling household items, and arranging them carefully, even things she knew should not have to be labeled, like the clock—a strip of tape pointing to 6 saying Sunday Bess Calls, a reminder to prepare for the weekly examination that her younger sister gave her by telephone from St. Louis. And with the script she noted the names of hardware and sports stores recommended by the uneasy clerks and managers, hoping they noticed, saw it as an instrument of clarity.

She finally obtained bullets from a man who did reloading for gun hobbyists, having prepared beforehand and neatly delivered to him the third lie of her life—excepting those she had told before her father's death and now told her sister every week to escape being sent to St. Louis. She had first lied regarding her age, in 1918, to a bemused dean of agriculture at the University of Missouri. He was disturbed partly by her youthful appearance and partly by the fact that she had walked the gravel turnpike twenty miles from Rocheport alone, but even more because she was a woman and he, against all regulation and sentiment, for no good reason either political or personal, was admitting her to the school of agriculture. The second lie was a continuation of the first: the age she noted on a teaching contract offered by the same dean four years later. And this, the third, was spoken simply, a few words that she had memorized for the man with bullets: "It is for my husband. He is a gun hobbyist."

*　　*　　*

Gripped by the memory of her father's potato-rough hand, her fingers trembled as the lever clicked shut, and she crept back to the window. Jewel purred loudly, nervously pacing the kitchen, and stroking against LaVerne's ankle. There was no movement visible now, although she seemed to discern tracks in the new snow leading from behind the woodpile to the house. The setting sun cast a deep orange light across the snow. "Fire before night," she whispered to herself.

She shifted her attention to the basement, where he had been coming into the house by night and recently by day. At night he waited until she had turned off her bedroom light and gone to bed. Usually he awakened her from the first drowse of sleep—the time, like waking, when her mind plunged through a miracle of crazy pictures—awakened her by the clinking of a spoon on Jewel's plate. Then he would move quietly across the hardwood floor, less in steps than the lifting of steps, sometimes into the hall and toward her room, through the doorway and to the foot of her bed. If already asleep, she felt his presence as a dream or a thing surrounding her dreams. At other times she was fully awake, hearing the slightly asthmatic rattle of his breath and imagining the slow blink of his yellow eyes. She would lie rigid in his presence rather than get up, for she had vowed not to do anything sudden or out of the ordinary that might result in a broken hip or leg. More than once she had lain without moving while he attacked Jewel.

It was the stench in the house that had finally driven her out for bullets—not for poison because Jewel might be the victim rather than the black tomcat, nor help from students who lived in the neighborhood because among them were foreigners and strange young men with beards—not these, but bullets for the rifle she had learned to shoot sixty years ago and never yet had reason to use. The stink was from the black tomcat. She scrubbed the floors with chemical disinfectant and shut Jewel's basement window, galled by this necessity since it was her custom to allow the animal free access outside. She had never doted on Jewel; they retained a distance that seemed mutually acceptable, the cat assuming the role of pet only at feeding times, when begging was necessary to remind the woman of her existence and need. The woman liked the animal as a farmer may like a worthless dog, less to fondle or prattle at or even watch than merely to coexist with, taking some enjoyment in the presence of other warm blood.

It irritated LaVerne when the cat rubbed against her leg. "Stop," she whispered, now listening at the basement door. It was irritating, too, to think of the basement, where several weeks ago the black tomcat had broken Jewel's shut window—as she imagined, hurling himself yellow eyes and face first through the solid pane of glass so that he could continue to bother her, an act confirming his strangeness, perhaps aberrance. Hearing the window break, she had taken the rifle and new bullets to the basement, there sat down in a lawn chair, which she had bought upon retiring and never used, and waited for the cat to show his face. The window had been broken from inside, indicating the tomcat had been locked in the basement when she shut Jewel's window three days before—locked *in*, not out. Waiting with the rifle, she imagined the cat pacing in darkness three days, ferreting for sustenance that did not exist in her clean basement, finally pushing, scratching on the place of light; then she saw—imagined—him back up, gather himself, and ram his whole weight against the glass, shattering it. No cat should do this.

Later she searched among shelves of labeled equipment for caulking compound and glass to fix the window. She found glass and a cutter but was unable to find the compound, and her determination to patch the window flagged as she began to lose herself among labels. Discovering boxes and cans of equipment that needed rearranging, she took them out and sat amidst the clutter with her tape and marker, intending to reshuffle it, once again to know exactly what was in her house. There were labels that puzzled her, boxes of things she did not remember putting away. On a shiny tin can the script—hers, unmistakably—read: Decorations, 4/10/68; inside were pinecones, nothing else, and she dumped them into the trash. A larger can, empty, was labeled Cherry Pie, 1/25/70. She ripped off the tape. The entire method of arrangement seemed strange, in fact impractical, and so she began anew the task of ordering things, moving from closet to closet and shelf to shelf, unpiling and emptying boxes and cans in the floor.

With cabinet nails that had been in storage since March 1942 and planks separately labeled 1 inch x 6 inches x 4 feet, she built new shelves in the utility closet. In the basement she pulled a standing shelf away from the wall so that it could be reached from both sides. She made lists and pored over them trying to establish the best plan, sitting at her old desk with sketches and outlines; the ink on her nib pen repeatedly drying as she tried to envision a perfect order—the more stubborn her determination, the more impossible the task. It was too much finally, not in physical quantity but in the meticulousness of her demands, and after several days of losing herself in traps of minuteness, falling into black holes between holes between things that had floated into nonsense, fearing that the cat would return and walk among her exposed things, sniff them, step on them or even worse, she abandoned her project and put things away as best she could.

There was no sound in the basement. She leaned the rifle in the corner, went out the back door and down the steps into the snow. Less concerned about small illnesses like colds and flu than certain larger things—accidents—LaVerne often, as now, neglected to put on her coat. At the woodpile she picked out three good logs, knocked the snow off, and carried them inside. She carried the weight easily. Back outside, she chopped kindling with a well-sharpened hatchet, her vigorous blows echoing into the silence of new snow. It was a blessing when snow made the student-infested neighborhood clean and quiet. Stopping and listening, she observed tracks around the house and followed them to the broken basement window. On all windows but this one she had placed storm fittings. She had leaned the last fitting against the wall and left the broken window open. Now she knew why. Carefully she bent over, gazing into the dark basement, and put the storm fitting into place. If he was in there now, he was trapped.

Back inside, she listened at the basement door, then shut it. After laying and setting a fire, she placed the screen in front of it and went into the bathroom. It was her birthday, and Sunday, and her sister would be calling around 6 P.M. She turned on the tub water and began taking off her clothes. A bath each Sunday relaxed and prepared her for the examination. Not that she was nervous— she was never so much that as steadily tense, vigilant—a quality that in recent years had forsaken her, or turned bad, as boundaries and delineations and even words themselves sometimes evaporated, and the vigilance lost center, turned in circles, becoming a blank dizzy tightness that wanted somehow to shatter. She always felt that way when her sister called and so took the soothing bath beforehand. In order to pass she had to keep her senses about her, answer the questions properly, and perhaps inquire about the grown nephews whose names she had taped onto the wall. It was just a friendly call. But she knew the stakes; her sister had made that clear.

She hung out a fresh towel and saw that the shade was securely drawn. She could not be too careful of her privacy, for strangely dressed young people walked across her property at all hours, presumably university students but often of such slovenly appearance, poor posture, and ragged clothing, that they seemed less students than poor farm children, offspring of sixty acres and antiquated techniques, of farms that refused or were unable to afford the benefits of science, like her own father's—children like those with whom she had gone to school in Rocheport before and during the Great War, who came to school streaked with mud and stinking of animals, went to sleep in class because they had been up doing chores since before sunrise, whose teeth turned green and sometimes broke off into their food. As a teacher she had fought rural mismanagement for forty-five years, and it disturbed her to see college students in the guise of poverty, all the worse since it was false. Dirty, unkempt young people loping across her yard were like ghosts out of that old time—false ghosts mocking the resolution and task of her life.

She ran hot water until the temperature was suitable, then carefully stepped into the tub. Warmth settled into her hips and legs as she lay back against the curve. Through the open door the living-room fire crackled. Jewel appeared, eyes wide, tail high, and began rubbing back and forth against the door frame. "Away!" She flicked water at the cat and it scampered out. She liked privacy in the bath. Hooking a green rubber hose onto the tap, she adjusted a moderate flow to keep the water warm, a gentle ruffle of pressure against her where the hose happened to rest.

The first noise in the basement did not register with LaVerne. She had already become unmoored, as she often did in the bath, without pause or transition breaking into pure reverie, a state no longer willed nor purely enjoyable but habitual, as if entering the tub turned some switch in her mind. It delighted and scared her, like the dreams she had had as a child before her father's death. She often thought of him—the image of him, as now, skating beside her down Penson's Creek at night, one month and two days before he was to get up from breakfast coughing, go outside to the woodpile, lean against it, and hemorrhage through the mouth—skating with the ease that he had learned as a young man in Chicago, a clerk who dreamed of mansions and empires and of courting rich young ladies, before he dropped it all and came back to a small farm in a dying town in mid-Missouri to live out his life—skating with his hands clasped behind, swaying rhythmically even as he rounded curves in the crooked frozen creek, his moon shadow a vague blur across the ice. He had bought the ice skates in Columbia, a full day's journey to and fro by wagon. Hers were two sizes small, but she did not complain. She jammed them onto her feet, amazed that he had gone off and bought them, had stomped in the front door at suppertime and handed them to her, demanding that she put them on. He paced the living room and coughed while she tied the laces. In twenty minutes they were out on Penson's Creek; her knock-kneed and stumbly, afraid that someone might see her; him worriedly explaining and demonstrating the basics of skating. She picked it up quickly, carried by the force of his will to have her suddenly *know* how to skate, whisking up behind and holding her, virtually lifting her from the ice and moving with her until her ankles were solid. Past the edge of town the creek widened and flowed through bottomland toward the Missouri River. Her father pointed at a slash of moon on the ice ahead of them and said, "Catch it!" Hurrying to keep up with him, she forgot to be awkward, leaned with him into the numb air, chasing the running white moon's reflection, no sound in the widening creek but the keening of their skates and his harsh breath. She strained to catch the moon, but then only to keep up with him, as the creek broadened and neared the river. It cracked around them and he headed her off. "Can't go no farther," he said. "We're too close now." They stood for a moment listening to the flow of the ice-choked river. Her father began to cough, and they headed back.

This time the noise was too loud not to register. She sat up very straight in the tub, the dream on her face becoming puzzlement. The sound repeated, echoed, as if to bring her back to now. Something very bad was happening, something breaking. She looked at the white enclosure around her, the fluid. Heat pressed uncomfortably against the inside of her thigh, where the green thing lay. Still confused, she reached out and turned knobs. Heat bloomed out of the green hose. Dark holes began to flare around her. She was standing. A thing ran across the floor in the other room.

She was dressed in something. She had a thought: I am dying. She held onto that thought but did not believe it. Now was the trial. She stood in the living-room doorway, looking at a thing above the fire. She looked at it until she understood what it was. It was her pet on the mantelpiece. "Jewel," she said. The couch spoke softness to her. Her legs were weak. But now was the trial that she had faced before, how many times she did not know, as around her little holes of darkness continued to burst. She stood in front of the wall clock in an effort to remember something, but its ticking seemed to slow down, its hands to slip. She acted.

The thing in her hands became a gun, and she leveled it, spitting a bullet onto the kitchen floor. She remembered that more were in it. Dizziness receding, she opened the basement door, turned on the lights, and started down the steps.

The animal was around her, claws against concrete, now flying through the shelf, arching, exploding in tin cans and jars out the other side, running against the wall and gone, hidden in a dark place. A can rolled in a circle and was still. Glancing through the litter, she felt herself slipping. "*You are a bad cat,*" she said out loud, startled by her own words. Approaching the other side of the basement, she held the gun ready to shoot. He was hiding under the other half of the house, where the basement ended and dirt lay within two feet of the floor joists. Her foot stung, evidently cut by a piece of broken glass, but she did not raise it for fear of losing her balance. She had not known that she was barefoot. The basement was a clutter. As the sting reached upward, her body became real, clarified, and the rifle settled into her hands, no longer an abstraction wielded like a stick in a dream but a rifle. It was cold. She realized that she was wet. At the concrete wall where the basement ended, she saw the cat. A moment before in frenzied movement, he now sat hunched in the dirt directly facing her about fifteen feet away, blinking his eyes lazily, apparently without fear. She could hear the slight rattle of his breath. She aimed at his face.

At that moment two things happened. The phone began to ring upstairs and she realized something: if the cat were shot under the floorboards she would not be able to get him out. It would be dangerous for her to clamber over the wall and through the dirt after him. But the phone was ringing quite insistently. She continued to aim at the cat's face. He seemed unconcerned. His yellow eyes blinked again, as if he were about to take a nap. It occurred to her that if she did not shoot him now she never would.

It was not in her nature to be indecisive, and so each moment longer—the ringing all in her ears—her irritation mounted toward decision. Now the cat did something strange. He got up and turned his back to her, then hunched down again. He looked up at the window that he had broken weeks before, now sealed by the storm fitting. It was dark outside. He was a big cat, well muscled but with a dull, ragged coat. She was aiming now at his back and the base of his upturned head. He seemed to be waiting for the window to open. Intervals between each ring of the phone got longer.

"You are a bad cat," she scolded, with one eye shut and the wooden stock against her cheek. She pulled the trigger not as her father had taught her but in a jerk, and the gun burst across the hollow space, in a single instant picking the cat up by the spine and snapping him in a perfect somersault. The shock of the explosion died into the ringing phone, and she tried to turn from the cat and go upstairs. On his back he wallowed spasmodically in the dirt, like a giant bug trying to flip himself over.

She turned and walked carefully through the litter toward the staircase. She would not run to catch the phone but would be careful, would hold the railing, and take each step at a time. And now at the bottom of the stairs, she would not falter at the sound—the dull thud that she heard behind her. But neither could she take the first step. There was no further sound—only the ringing phone upstairs—but she knew something was wrong. A terrible, sweet weakness loosened in her chest and spread. She smelled her father's breath, suffused with the odor of the black liquid that he carried in a bottle in his pocket during the last months and sometimes drank to giddiness. She was astonished by him when he got that way, when he laughed at dinner, coughed and laughed, mumbling that he was dying and then laughing more—a grotesque joke that made her and the younger sisters laugh, too, they who were old enough by then—or who lived in a time when at their age they could know—that he was not merely joking. And him tickling her with his rough, snub hands, the only part of him that was the same, the rest an impersonation by someone younger than her father who grinned strangely and seemed, at the last, a little silly.

Now she heard a quick shallow rattle of breathing behind her. She turned and was not surprised to see the cat walking across the basement floor toward her. He came sideways, his rear feet advancing independently of his forefeet. His head down like a mule in harness, he approached her. LaVerne tried to cock the rifle. But then the cat's rear feet walked faster, and he turned in a circle and sat down among shards of glass. His back and part of his head were exploded, ridiculously unzipped. He fell onto his side and shuddered, was for a moment still, then reached out with one paw, stretching his claws and slowly pulling inward as if to bring something to himself.

The phone had stopped ringing. LaVerne walked carefully, right foot and right foot, up the stairs. In the kitchen she put the rifle into its cloth. On the couch in the living room she sat down. Jewel stared brightly at her from the mantelpiece. She waited for the fire to warm her. The phone would ring soon, and she began to prepare for her sister, the tiny irritating voice that would jabber from the receiver. She thought of what she would say. The cat continued to stare at her, making her uncomfortable. She looked at the cut on her foot. It needed care. Her glance fidgeted around the room and then up again at the wide-eyed cat.

3

JACK WOMAN KILLER

JOE was Grandfather for the meeting, and he required that it be held in a teepee. A teepee, with nothing but a field of dead popcorn stalks between it and the November wind, was not pleasant to sit in all night, no matter how good the medicine or how warm the fire. The fire was generous, as always, winter or summer, when tended by Billy Caulder, a short bedraggled hipless man whose pants generally looked like they were about to fall down. He worked slowly around the fire without faltering, getting smoke in his nose and sneezing, grimacing, and shielding his face, but always with such monotonous certainty of movement that he seemed irritated and hypnotized at once. All night, Jack's front baked while his back froze against the tent canvas. For relief, he finally asked Grandfather for a fourth dose of medicine. Energy rode Jack's spine like high-volt power, making him want to go out and chase rabbits under the new moon, and he was seeing snakes in the fire.

Grandfather refused a fourth dose. Jack asked for the medicine tea, and Grandfather refused that, too.

It was the first time he had ever seen Grandfather refuse anyone in a meeting, and that was disturbing. Jack had come to think of "asking Grandfather" as a mere formality to which old Joe always simply nodded his vague yes. Yes to go outside to the bathroom, yes to speak, yes to sing out of turn, yes to take more medicine—yes in an unhurried fire-lit gauzy-eyed nod as he sat motionless, hunched around eighty-five or ninety years.

Joe was ornery lately. It was ornery of him to require that this meeting be held in a teepee. It was a thank-you event for Rosie Raskin, who had come back to life after three days in a Tulsa hospital with her temperature up to 106 degrees. Rosie was here for the meeting, but she didn't look all that good. By the time the midnight water had been passed and the drum had started around a second time, she looked to Jack about as healthy as a marshmallow, and he doubted that she'd make it through the night without coming down sick again. The meeting should have been held in a house. Rosie didn't ask to speak, but her husband stood twice and gave talks in which he thanked the spirit for bringing her back. In the second talk he broke down and wept, and people in the circle uttered "yes, yes" to the spirit that could enter in these moments.

Jack was not with it though. He became aloof. He watched Grandfather, and refused the drum when it came around the second time. Mario, who sat to his left and would have sung if Jack had taken the drum, leaned over, and whispered, "Biting your tail, Jack. Watch out, too much medicine makes you go in circles."

"I'm cold," Jack said.

Mario pulled back. "So you want the Medal of Honor?" Mario prided himself on being a realist, tougher minded than an Indian. He was from the South Bronx, which he characterized as making Harlem look like a model neighborhood. "Packs of wild dogs come out at night in the South Bronx," he would say. "They're more dangerous than wolves." He sometimes kidded Jack for having gone to Harvard. "I just wonder, Jack, did you get the idea to be a janitor at Harvard?" One night when they were out drinking, Jack answered him, "No, Mario, I got the idea to be a janitor the same way you got the idea to be such a witty conversationalist—drinking beer at the Starlight Road Inn."

Most of the older church members disapproved of heavy drinking, but if Grandfather Joe did, he expressed it only through certain silences. A couple of times Jack had tested him with jokes about drinking, but Grandfather paid no attention. A good number of church members did their share of it. Frank Raskin himself, here tonight to thank the spirit for his wife's life, popped tops at the Starlight a good four nights a week.

Jack tried to forget Grandfather's refusal and get into the meeting. There were two unfamiliar faces in the circle, a suntanned hippy with a Navajo serape and a middle-aged man who had been wringing his hands and crying since before the second turn of the drum. The crying man asked permission to speak, stood up, and said that he came from Tulsa, where he lived in utter misery. Haltingly, he explained that he was a floor man for Sears, and that over the past several years he had violated three of his daughters and, what was worse, couldn't stop violating two of them. Although he lived in the church capital of the world and had at one time or another gone to just about all of them for a solution to this agony, it hadn't done any permanent good, and he had come to this Indian church as a last resort, and he hoped in the name of Christ that it would help to chew this bitter root and drink this bitter draught, and that he could return home and be a decent father to his family.

While the man talked, no one in the circle said "yes" or the quiet "uh-huh, uh-huh" that meant go on and speak it out, we are your witnesses. The man stood hunch shouldered in a white shirt and thin tie with a pearl tiepin, speaking into the circle of faces, some dim eyed and staring into the fire, others watching him and looking down, watching, glancing down, with the delicacy that had always seemed to Jack more country poor than Indian, among folk who had started learning the art of white embarrassment two hundred and more years ago. To Jack, it was one of a dozen ways that the Easterners were not really Indians at all and had not been for at least the span of Grandfather Joe's life. Some still referred to their blood—Choctaw, Cherokee, Creek, Seminole, Chickasaw— but they reminded Jack of Southerners still pretending to be Confederates. They were all breeds now, and virtually since they had been sent to this land, enough of them had succeeded at being white men (with cotton, slaves, oil, soybeans, and the rest) that it was less a tribe that defined a person than an economic class.

The people of this church were mostly poor, and they were

embarrassed by the Tulsa man's story but not surprised. It was not unusual for a desperate stranger to find his way into a meeting and go wild on the medicine. Because the people were embarrassed, they did not speak out to encourage him on. He was now describing how it had all started when he began having ungodly dreams about his daughters. The kind of talk they were likely to encourage was not sensational like this, not a good Baptist confession, but a ritual witness, some kind of gratitude or need that could be shared by them all. Life, health, sanity, the continuity of a marriage. There was a pattern: after asking "Grandfather, can I say something?" a speaker stood and puffed on a hand-rolled cigarette and began to thank the spirit or make a request in phrases that were short, repetitive, inelegant, puffing the smoke, phrases that began to fall apart, the same few words spoken ten, fifteen, twenty times, until they came from the chest and stomach, broken into pieces. During his first meetings, fresh back from college, Jack thought that they sounded like senile professors who had forgotten their lectures and refused to sit down. It was painful. After a few weeks, he began to see that the talks were an attempt to reach and share an attitude of spirit, not to sermonize or reveal something new. Yet even with the medicine, that sharing was not easy, and frequently the speaker would stand and burn his lips on the tobacco and despite encouragement from around the circle, never quite find the breath of concurrence.

There were no judgments made on the talks, although a real one—when a speaker found his need or thankfulness, and for a moment beyond pride became it—this was remembered and discussed after meetings like a good rawhide drum or fine medicine. Jack liked to listen to the old ones tell about talks they heard in an oil town thirty years ago, or talks that went back even farther and were remembered second and third hand. Jack had himself spoken only a few times and never to ask something for himself. He took the drum when it made the circle, but he had never sung.

To Jack, meeting in a teepee always seemed a little strange. For the Civilized Tribes, so long under white influence, a teepee was about as natural as it might be to a Kiwanis Club banquet. And when they chanted and beat the drum, it sometimes seemed like Indians in an old movie.

The man from Tulsa continued to describe his sins. Jack leaned over to Mario and whispered, "Grandfather should cut him off. He said no to me, he can say no to this creep."

Mario whispered back, "Yeah, I did it with my cousin in the South Bronx for years. Big deal—she's got a happy family now. You're biting your tail, though, Jack. Don't bite your tail."

"What do you mean? This guy's a creep. Grandfather can damn sure tell him to sit down." Jack's voice was a little too loud now. Wade Peters, who was acting as road man, looked at him from across the tent.

Mario paused, then leaned back. "The medicine can go sour. You have to watch out. That's why Grandfather said you couldn't have no more."

"To hell with it. My back is cold; Rosie Raskin looks like shit on a shingle . . . Joe should never have called this meeting in a tent. So we sit up all night freezing our butts off, listening to this creep." A fist of energy built in Jack's spine. His ribs hummed like neon tubes. He felt mean as a sow. He felt as if he could stand up and make the tent topple over like a paper cup in wind. He could dive into the fire and swim like a muskrat. He could break the Tulsa creep's bones.

The skinny tie hung like a black noodle from the creep's neck. ". . . and then I started laying for her, I guess you'd say—now this is the youngest one, Mary Dee, I'm talking about now. I'd come home and stand outside the bathroom door listening for the poor little thing in there, doing her bu'ness there, you know. Poor little Mary Dee couldn't hardly take a wee wee without me up against the door listening and seeing things in my own mind that I swear they would have put me in jail and threw away the key for. When the poor thing had to do number two, I'd walk in on her and pretend to brush my teeth or some such. Once I got her to take a bath with me. Bubble bath, oh help me Lord, wasn't nobody else in the house, and I lured Mary Dee in there with a bubble bath. Truth of the matter was, something terrible was being hid by them bubbles. As if I hadn't already done enough to my poor family. Blue bubbles they was. . . ."

Jack was getting more and more irritated. This guy was getting his back up real seriously. At first he felt heavy, dead, thick in his body, but the more the man talked, the more jerky he felt. Now he felt dead tired and jerky and cold, which added up to something like Frankenstein. Or a bull in the charge stall with two hundred volts shooting through him and the door bolted shut. He was ready to break something. The fire was unreal and gave off no heat. The faces watching the skinny man were abashed, cowardly. "Shut up," Jack said. No response: no one spoke those words in a meeting. Jack said it again, half aware that he was speaking. "*Shut up, you creep.*" Everyone heard this time, even the speaker. Then Jack was up and walking through the fire and picking up the man like he had two handles on him. The man did not squirm or resist. Outside, he threw him down like a log onto the dirt. "Get out of here, mister. Take your shit jive back to Tulsa and give it to Oral Roberts."

Jack went back inside the tent and took his place, heart pounding. When he looked up, Billy Caulder was poking the fire back together, and everybody else was frozen stiff as statues. Some of them were looking at him big eyed. There was a good minute of silence inside the tent. Outside, the man sniffled off, and a car door opened and shut. Wade Peters came between Jack and the fire. "Should I take him out, Grandfather?"

"No," Grandfather croaked. He cleared his throat and repeated clearly, "No."

"You want me to do anything?" Wade asked.

"Yes," Grandfather said. "Go out there and hold that man. Take him into Frank's house and give him coffee. He can't go out on the highway with the medicine."

"Would you do that, Frank?" Wade asked. "I believe I should stay here."

Someone next to Rosie Raskin took up the drum and shook

the water and pebbles around inside it, preparing the rawhide.

"Stop the drum," Grandfather Joe said. "We have to talk now."

Jack was sitting in his place, heart rattling like a diesel. "You're going to have to cool it," Mario said. "You're not the only one here."

"Be quiet with Jack," Grandfather said. He had not changed his posture—one elbow on a knee, one leg in the dirt. His voice returned to the usual hoarse whisper, scarcely loud enough to be heard across the tent. "Do you want to speak, Jack?"

"I've spoken."

"Unh." Grandfather grinned through his three teeth. "What are you—Geronimo?"

A moment of silence, then Wade Peters laughed out loud, one big "Haw!" Someone else laughed, then they were all laughing. Jack saw their faces for the first time tonight. Will Goodman who owned the Dairy Queen and looked like a perpetual heart-attack victim. Leona Goodman with her face fallen more on one side than the other. Johnny Bell, eighteen years old and God's gift to Briartown. Flo Ann and Amos Manley, popcorn farmers with last year's drought etched even in their laughter. George Padgett, an ageless bum who hung around Eufala and somehow never starved. Franklin Elliott, fishing guide and boat renter, who seldom talked, at least to Jack, and who owned the farm where this meeting was being held. Billy Erwin who had graduated from Norman and travelled around the world on one thousand dollars flat and, according to his own story, smoked opium in Afghanistan and run over a shoeshine boy on a borrowed B.M.W. outside New Delhi—incidents that Jack had heard Billy tell so many times at the Starlight Road Inn that he no longer believed them. Maggie Black who waited tables at a twenty-four-hour truck stop on the interstate and wore her hair scorched blonde in a perilous bouffant high above her flat Seminole face. These and about fifteen others, all of whom Jack knew in one way or another, through scraps of gossip and the feeling they gave off in meetings if not through personal acquaintance. Jack knew them from high school or the Starlight or town business or hunting dove on their land or any one of a dozen other ways. They laughed at him inside the smoky cold tent on the November ground, while Grandfather sat there in the firelight with his smile melting down into the openmouthed stare that could have been wisdom or could have been senility, Jack was never quite sure.

He was not proud of the fact that he had just broken up the meeting. His body still jerked with the strange voltage—thighs, belly, and chest—but softening now into something less and less unpleasant. He felt mean and right, jittery and ashamed. Everything was in two pieces: the power in his spine cut up the middle and cleaved his sight in two. He could stay or leave, it didn't make a damn. He could walk out and get into his pickup and be in Texas by noon, or he could stay here and put up with this bunch, all of their sad laughing faces. Maynard Windfree, an old Caddo, stout as a potato, was the only one who remained serious.

Grandfather stared directly at Jack. "So you don't want to talk. You want me to talk?"

"You can talk. Any damn time you want to."

"Okay," Grandfather said, "I'll ask you what the man inside wants."

"What man?"

"Inside you."

Laughter and whispers died away.

"The man inside me wants this meeting not to be taken over by stupid creeps."

"That's not the man."

Jack muttered, "You going to be wise, Grandfather?"

The old man's smile showed two snaggleteeth. "If I can."

Jack felt off balance and mean, as if he had done some terrible thing, ventured some wild commitment. The peyote, which the old man had denied him more of, was like bitter clear light in his veins. "What are we supposed to do here, run a freak show?"

"If we have freaks," Grandfather said.

"Well bring the bastards on. Maybe we can put advertisements out on the interstate."

A hand grabbed him. "Look Jack, don't . . . ."

He pulled loose. "Let go of me, Mario—buddy—don't mess with me right now."

Billy Caulder added a couple of sticks and poked the fire, as if nothing unusual was going on. Grandfather continued, "It's my place to tell you that you can't throw a person out. I've been going to meetings for a long time. You don't come here to judge. You come to give thanks and ask the spirit to be with you. You sing and talk, and if there's a lie in what you say, you're more likely to figure it out on your own than by being told."

"You're telling me I did something wrong."

"You did."

The energy lifted Jack by the shoulders, as if to pull him to his feet. There were a lot of things he could do now, and he saw the possibilities going down like cards.

"Look Grandfather," Wade Peters said, "if you want me to take Jack out and stay with him, I will. I think the medicine has knocked him loony tonight."

Jack hoped that Wade Peters didn't try to take hold of him. He didn't have anything against Wade, but he wasn't going to be pushed around by anybody on any account right now. Whatever he did next, he would decide for himself.

"No," Grandfather said, still looking into the fire.

People whispered. Johnny Bell spoke half aloud, "He can't take on like that in a meeting. Just 'cause he went off to college." "It's hateful," someone hissed. Maggie Black looked thoughtful and tense, the frozen thicket of blonde above her face quivering slightly. "Taken on a fit, if you ask me," Will Goodman said. "I had a kid at the Dairy Queen last summer take on a fit, like to took the place apart. Busted somebody's nose, chased the girls out from behind the counter, and ate dairy cream directly from the machine. . . ."

Grandfather was silent until their murmuring had died away. "Now, Jack Woman Killer, you'll let us have the meeting."

The statement was not as strange to Jack as the use of his name. Grandfather so seldom called you by even your first name. He wanted to reply, "Sure I'll let you have it, why should I interfere? Nothing wrong with a few milk brain idiots sitting around in a teepee on Saturday night beating on a drum. Get on with it." But he didn't. Instead, he said something else, unintended. He heard himself say it.

"The name stinks. Why don't you give me a new one?"

*   *   *

The name, after all, had a lot to do with it—with everything. It was how he had gotten into Harvard. His high-school grades and test scores were so low that there had been some question as to whether he would be admitted at Norman, or even Stillwater, and on an inspiration he hitchhiked to Cambridge and talked to an assistant admissions director at Harvard. That was in 1966. The assistant admissions director took Jack out to lunch and asked him about his background. Jack told him that he had played left halfback for Eufala High School, and his senior year they had won an Oklahoma regional championship. He told him that he had raised sheep. "Sheep?" the assistant admissions director repeated, somewhat interested. "I had thirty head." "What is your racial background?" the assistant director asked. "Mostly Cherokee," Jack said, "but my father's father was Sac and Fox." "Sac and what?" "The Sac and Fox was a very small tribe. They lived on a little strip in the western territory. Others hated them because of the cannibalism." "What cannibalism?" "Yes sir. My grandfather denied that they did it in recent times, but back in the old days they maybe ate some people. I think it was just on special occasions, though. The other tribes hated them, and they had it pretty rough. My father says there are sixty-eight Sac and Fox left in the world, and three of them live in Hong Kong. My name, I guess, is Sac and Fox."

"And you say your name is Jack Woman Killer." "Yes sir." "How do you spell that?" "J-a-c-k W-o-m-a-n K-i-l-l-e-r." "You're in." "Sir?" "I said you're in. Full scholarship. Come back to the office, and I'll get you through."

That was how Jack got into Harvard. It had been nice there for four years. He didn't have to do anything special to keep in school, so he spent a lot of time smoking marijuana and chasing girls. He found himself more successful at this when he changed his name to Man Killer, since a number of young ladies responded to his real name as if he was trying to make a bad joke. "Oh yeah? Well my name is Peter Peckers, see you around, Jack."

His fourth year at Harvard, Jack turned away from the social life and became introspective. He began to worry about who he was and what he would do when he graduated. The only course he had flunked at Harvard was Southwestern American History, so he decided to become a historian specializing in Southwestern America. It didn't work out. He majored in history, all right, but his grades weren't high enough for graduate school. Now, several years out of college, he was living twenty-five miles from where he had grown up and working as a "maintenance supervisor" for highway rest stops.

He had tried San Francisco for a while. There he determined to call himself "Jack Smith," but every time he did so, he got a stomachache and felt weak all over. After a few weeks as "Jack Smith," he tried turning his real name around backwards. That gave him less pain in the gut, but among potential employers "Jack Namow Rellik" caused as much suspiciousness as his true name, especially when they asked what "kind" it was, and he had to explain that it was Sac and Fox. It seemed that every time he told about the tribe, he could not help but go on and mention their reputed cannibalism. Perhaps he did this because of the amazing success he'd once had in explaining it to the assistant admissions director. Or perhaps he couldn't help mentioning it because that was the only thing he knew about the tribe. His father had talked about them during Jack's childhood, but he seldom listened. The only other solid thing he knew about them was from a daguerreotype in his Southwestern American History text at college, which showed members of the tribe standing around outside a mud hut. They were very short, squat men with fat brown faces, wearing buffalo robes, and some with horned buffalo helmets. There was one white man in the picture, who looked like a grown-up among fat-faced children at a dress-up party. Jack quit telling potential employers that the name was Indian and began claiming that it was Polish, but his stomach kept hurting when he did.

After a few months in the Bay Area, he came back home, got the maintenance job with the state, joined the church, and resigned himself to living in a place where he wouldn't have to make up a name. What had he found back home, though? Billy Erwin at the Starlight telling his story for the umpteenth time about how he travelled around the world on one thousand dollars flat. And the name had a lot to do with it. The very name itself.

*   *   *

Grandfather wasn't responding. He was waiting.
Jack spoke at his feet. "I want a new name."
"How will you do it?" Grandfather asked.
"Anything's possible. Give me a new name."
"Oh Jesus," Mario said. "Look man . . . ."
Jack looked directly at Grandfather. "You give me a name."
Grandfather searched his shirt pocket and patted his pants. He looked up. "I didn't bring any extras."
"Call me Jack Smith."
"What will I do with your old name?"
"Hock it in Tulsa."
Someone giggled. Others shifted and muttered among themselves. They were surprised, some irritated. There was more confusion, and Grandfather seemed for a moment to go to sleep in the

fire. "Grandfather, can I say something?" It was Maggie Black. She stood up. "Well I was just going to say, I don't blame him. We got a girl at the I. P. by the name of Chlorine. That's her Christian name, and she hasn't got no middle name like Sue or Jean to use so she can drop Chlorine, and, what I mean, she gets more trouble out of that thing than out of a seventy-five-cent bust. They wrastle her raw some nights on the speed shift, asking her if she's been swimming lately and carrying on with the same old limp jokes until you'd think they had done come together and *decided* to drive her up the wall. She takes it real good, but here she is eighteen years old and looking like she's thirty-eight and done had six kids and give up. It's the name, pure and simple. I told her that, too, so I ain't talking behind her back. I said she ought to just take her little self right down to the courthouse and get rid of that silly thing and take on something decent. Her father was probably drunk when he give it to her anyway. I don't see why a person has to carry around a name worse than a gimp leg when all they have to do is change it." Maggie sat down, arranged herself, and checked her bouffant. The circle murmured and shifted. Maynard Windfree blew his nose.

Billy Erwin spoke up, somewhat prissily, "If I had a name like Jack's, I'd thank the spirit for my good luck."

Flo Ann whispered to Amos Manley, "You remember Violet Buzzard?"

Mario stood up. "Look, in New York . . . ."

"Ask Grandfather before you talk!" Wade Peters boomed. Wade was one of those who was irritated.

Before Mario could get started, Franklin Elliott appeared through the tent flap, face red as a beet. "I need some help with this character out here. I got him in the house, and he's already broken my portable TV and tried to scorch himself with hot coffee. I got him hobbled now, but I need help."

Grandfather gave Will Goodman and Johnny Bell the eye, and they left with Franklin. The circle whispered and muttered. Wade Peters was getting more irritated. Even Maynard looked a little on edge. Meetings seldom got confused like this. Only Billy Caulder, tending the fire, seemed undisturbed.

Jack heard himself say it again, "Give me a name."

Grandfather finally cleared his throat. He looked into the fire. "I can't do magic here. I sing and try to find the spirit, but no magic. Your name is Jack Woman Killer. You have western blood, I guess. . . ." His voice faded out again as he stared into the fire.

Jack was standing. He felt strong and correct. The choice that he had muddled over and avoided all these years was suddenly clear. It was incredibly obvious. He couldn't believe that he hadn't simply done it. Thousands of people all over the country had taken on names like Sweet Grass and Dancing Bear and Shakti Das; and all he wanted was a good stout Jones or Smith. It was simple and clear, and this moment, this November night in this popcorn field, was the time to do it.

"A name," he said aloud.

Grandfather looked up at him, elbow on one knee, other knee in the dirt. He did not seem to be in as much hurry as Jack. "I've known lots of western names. I'd be proud to have one."

"I'll trade you."

Grandfather smiled again. "Unfair. I'd bury yours before it had a good chance."

"God knows it's time," Jack said.

"What is his name?" the hippy with the serape asked. Someone told him, and he stared over at Jack. "Far fucking out."

Wade Peters exploded. "Out. Get out. You get out of here with your dirty talk!" He started to eject the hippy, but Grandfather intervened.

"No, no. The drum has been stopped. We're talking now. It's okay."

"Ain't okay to me," Peters muttered. "Talking dirty in church." But he deferred to Grandfather.

Jack took a step forward.

Grandfather hesitated. "The meeting was for Rose Raskin, to give thanks for her health. Maybe we can ask her what she thinks."

Rose was shy. She hemmed and hawed and finally said. "I just don't know. I've seen lots of interesting names, but I never would have thought to change them. I had a friend, name of Scott Tree, when I was growing up. And there was someone, name of White Snow, over in Eufala. . . ."

"Honey, that's a laundry detergent," said Leona Goodman gently.

"I knew somebody in Fort Smith named Ima Hogg," Maggie offered.

Billy Erwin spoke up, "You wouldn't believe the names in India."

"The one that was accused of killing Belle Starr, what was his name?"

"Blue Duck," answered Billy Caulder, poking at the fire.

"So what's the big deal?" Mario said. "We could read a Bronx phone directory and laugh for ten years."

Jack was irritated by the chatter. He wanted to get on with it. A swell of righteousness came over him. His heart beat like a hammer in his chest. The name had to be banished like the ridiculous burden that it was, and the old man sitting limply in the dirt before him could do it now simply and quickly. He had the age, the gravity, the good sense. He would provide the words. The agreement. The acceptance.

"Why don't you just go over to Tahlequah, honey?" Leona said. "They could probably do it there in the courthouse."

"I want it now."

George Padgett spoke up. "Have you ever tried using the first part of the name as an initial. Maybe that wouldn't sound bad. Jack W. Killer."

This caused another outburst of opinion. "That sounds worse." "I don't know, at least it isn't so specific." "Well, if somebody that called himself Jack Killer came to the D.Q. asking for a job, I'd give it to him; maybe he'd take care of some of them smart alecks peeling out in my driveway and throwing beer cans. . . ."

"What do you say?" Jack cut off the chatter.

Grandfather still looked into the fire. "We can talk about it. I can't change your name, but we can talk about it together."

"I don't want to talk about it, I want to change it." Jack took a big breath. He felt like a grown-up explaining something obvious to a child. "Look, if you were living in a city somewhere, and an Eskimo came up to you wearing sealskins and fur and the whole outfit, and he said, 'I need some help, everybody's staring at me and I feel uncomfortable; what can I do?' Wouldn't you maybe suggest that he change his clothes? Wouldn't that be a decent thing to do?"

"A name isn't clothes," said Grandfather.

Wade Peters and several others were very uncomfortable at what was going on. Meetings were not supposed to be discussion sessions: the taking of medicine, the drum, the singing, even the "talk" were formal events. Hank was among those who were uncomfortable, yet he was the instigator. He wanted it to be over and done with. He was committed to it being done. "A name. Then we can sing or something. . . ."

Grandfather glanced up at him. His voice was almost a whisper. "Jack. This is the Native American Church. I have been in it since before the First World War. We've had many bad times. Years ago they tried to do away with us because we weren't 'Christian,' as they understood us. They tried to banish us because of the medicine. For years the meetings had no more than five or six people. I have been to meetings where there were only two of us. At other times, when the crops were bad year after year, hundreds tried to join. People took medicine outside of meetings and tried to perform magic to bring back the crops. To abolish the curse on the land. We decided at that time that we would perform no magic. We decided that our purpose was to find the spirit, not to change the world. I have been to meetings when the dust blew so hard all night that the light bulbs in the house were like dim eyes, and we could not see each other's faces, and in tent meetings where the fire could not be kept burning. Yet we agreed not to beg the spirit."

"I don't want to beg the spirit. I want a name—a word." Jack

43

was angry. His hands were in fists. The medicine made it seem simple. Why was he asking this old man? Why was he listening to his croaking pieties?

Grandfather replied, but his voice had died out completely. It had happened before in other meetings, his mouth working with no sounds coming out. Maynard leaned over and whispered into his ear, and Grandfather took a drink of medicine tea from the pickle jar. He rolled a cigarette and cleared his throat. "I believe in change. But I get lost and confused when I mix that with the meetings. I don't know—that may be my fault. . . . But when you perform magic you are looking to the outside."

"What is prayer?" Jack asked.

"Prayer is humble," the old man said.

"Give me a humble name."

"You have spoken of Tulsa. You're right. Tulsa is where Christians learn to be better Christians so that they can get richer. They go to God so that He will raise their salaries. It is very hard to understand this—it took me more years than I would like to admit—but you must not confuse the spirit with the other. When you do, it can become a force of evil. The churches in Tulsa are greedy. They have confused God with the world. They build the world into their churches. Their priests are wizards."

"What does that have to do with my name?"

"I am telling you why I do not perform in these meetings. Only seek."

"Is this what the cactus teaches?"

Grandfather looked up at him, the suggestion of a smile at the corner of his mouth and in his eyes. "You believe now—at this moment—that anything is possible, don't you, Jack? The medicine has given you that power."

"You're catching on." The words shook out of him. He could not look into Grandfather's face.

"Then I'll try to sing," the old man said, "a test of your faith."

Green wood in the fire crackled as the drum and staff came around. By unspoken agreement, Maynard Windfree always took

44

the drum when Grandfather sang. He got up with the drum and stood for a moment while blood came into his legs. He was a bulky man who had worked construction most of his life. His face was inexpressive leather. Maynard moved next to Joe, sat down, and sloshed water in the drum to wet the skin. He held staff against drum, and after a moment began to find a rhythm. Grandfather's song was no different from the one he gave in the mornings, at the last of meetings when all in the circle would reach out and open their palms, and the sun would come clear on the ground and take over the fire. His voice was too old to be fine, but at a level higher than his talking voice it still had something left to it. Jack had never heard Grandfather sing except at sunrise.

As always it was short. When he had finished, there was no hint of daybreak through the smoke hole. Jack stood and was only vaguely aware that Mario grabbed him by an ankle and tried to hold him. He walked halfway around the circle before stopping. Shoulders slumped, he spoke without turning, "Grandfather, may I leave?"

Then it was as if the bones in his own head whispered. "I'm an old man. In my whole life I haven't travelled as far as you, Jack Woman Killer. Sometimes my mind goes blank, and I know nothing. But I sing for you and what is possible in your life."

Jack's spine was stiff. "May I leave?" he repeated.

Through the sound of the fire he heard the old man's whisper.

4

MOMMA AND THE MOONMAN

HOME from work two hours early, Roselle dropped her coat onto the bed and went to the bathroom for some pain reliever. Her image in the mirror swelled, blurred to a puddle, and she touched her head gingerly, in disbelief, feeling her temple and forehead to make sure this thing was for real. Her head felt like a big rotten pumpkin. Momma's nerve capsules were spilled across the counter, and she took a handful, plus a half-dozen aspirin, and washed them down.

In the living room her husband Olin was stretched out asleep on the couch with his old brown working hat balanced on his nose and forehead, and Momma was watching TV. Roselle sat down and spoke to Momma, but her head was such a mess that at first she didn't understand the answer. Momma clicked her teeth impatiently and repeated herself. "Lif' off. They goin' to the moon. Ain't you heard, child?" Momma blinked—her hard bright eyes penetrated by black pins of light. "I switch on for As the World Turn and has you got troubles with yo' regularity, and what do I see but three moonmens. Child, they goin' to the moon in place of my story." Roselle tried to get Momma in focus. The left side of her head felt heavy and swollen, like a boil close to popping, and arcs of pain bloomed against her skull.

Momma jumped out of her chair and chanted, "*White mens, white mens / Flyin' to the moon / Get yo' butt / out of my room.*"

Roselle winced. "Have you been into your medicine, Momma?"

"I ain't taken no medicine, child, 'cept what the doctor order, millions of tiny time-release capsules—but hush! I must get that trash outen the TV, make room for my story. *Moonmens, moonmens* . . . ."

"Why ain't Olin at work?" Roselle held the aching side of her head. Weak and sick at her stomach, she didn't have the energy to put up with this. She repeated slowly, "Why is Olin here 'stead of at Mr. Jack's workin'?"

"I ain't studyin' Olin. *Moonmens in the sky / Listen here to me / I might be colored / but get off my TV.*" Momma approached the television and swept her arms as if to force the picture off the screen.

A rocket steamed in the background, while an announcer spoke tiny sounds that pulsed through Roselle's head. He seemed to be building up to something. ". . . result of fifteen years and thirty-five . . . governmental and contractual . . . and just a few years ago the charismatic German born . . . Saturn Stage-One Rocket . . . what was considered a primitive fuel base, kerosene, and . . . the brain weighs a total of 4,625 . . . thrust of 7.5 million . . . million automobiles running simultaneously . . . first stage alone, eight thousand feet of . . . X-rayed and hand . . . ."

Momma stared dreamily at Roselle. "It's a shame, child. You don't know what kind of fix these white folks is into. Roberta done got thrown into jail 'cause Suzanne, Mr. Jim's sec'tary, found a letter said she was sufferin' from what they call 'nesia, which makes her forgetful, and she done been married to three mens without knowin'—'magine that! Now Suzanne went right to the district attorney and told on Roberta—he's an old slickedy dude with puffy eyes—and he put her behind bars befo' you could say jackrabbit. Course, Suzanne, she had her own reasons—mainly that a good while ago she started in courtin' Mr. Jim, despite he was supposed to be married to Roberta. Now Roberta—she's a sweet thing—she's behind bars, and Jim can't visit 'cause he have a heart-attack break-down from hearin' she done got around so smart with that many mens. Mrs. Olson come boil her coffee sometime and the Avon lady come a'dingdong to sell her blush powder now and again, but mostly she sit alone and look grey in the face. Now that old sec'tary, I don't trust her! She's been comin' to the hospital and makin' up to Jim, sittin' next to his bed readin' the Scripture till he go to sleep, po' thing, and she close the Scripture and look down at him real satisfied—'bout like a floozie if you ask me."

"Oh Momma."

T minus 11.

Momma looked sternly at her daughter. "Roselle, has you got rid of that unsightly bathtub ring yet? Now leave me to my story, soon as I get these rocket bombs out. Silly mens done brung all them folks from oversea to speculate how to burn kerosene. Po' Roberta should be at the courthouse now findin' out which of these husbands she married to. *Moonmens, boo! / Jump outen that box / 'Less I get you out / By tyin' some knots.*"

Roselle gazed blankly at the TV, waiting for the medicine to take effect. The scene had shifted to one of the moonmen: angle shot of a ballooning light-colored suit with straps, bags, and plumbing fixtures hanging off every whichaway, a zippered white canister with tinted fishbowl visor, and one arm that looked about ten feet long reaching toward the camera-playing switches, while the mouth inside the globe spoke letters and numbers across Roselle's living room, into her headache. Momma was chanting and Baptist-cussing the man, just like he was here listening.

The sound was turned way down. Lately Momma liked it that way. Turned up, she claimed it hurt her ears, and besides it was her story, she didn't need nobody to tell her what was going on. Likely as not, that was true, for she had been watching the same Little Rock station on the same Magnavox since she went nuts eighteen years ago and probably by now was the world's living expert. These days, she had been watching it even more: from breakfast on through quiz and talk shows, afternoon movies and her story, up past news and prime-time programs, right on through late shows to the test pattern—the Indian bull's-eye that had since 1955, without fail, put her right to sleep, at which time Olin would grumblingly tote her to the toilet and run the faucet, then take and lay her out like a bag of sticks on the bed. Covering Momma up, Roselle sometimes stayed and listened to her sleep talk: weary long stitches of quiz questions, weather reports, wild Indians, bowling, football, Japanese monsters, I Love Lucy, Divorce Court, Oral Roberts, Little Rock Close-Up, Secret Storm, used car, rug, savings-loan, magic-mincer, and constipation advertisements—all holding her tense, making her to wind around in her sheets and kick like a dog dreaming of rabbits.

Now lately it had gotten worse. She talked along with the announcer when the sound was off, putting the exact words into his mouth. She blinked her eyes each time the scene shifted, never in between. Somehow she knew when it was going to shift, even these crazy new shows where it changed every breath you took. She would look at a program five minutes and have the shifting figured: blink . . . blink. . . . There were other things that Roselle didn't understand or really want to: chanting, faces she'd make, orders she'd give, sometimes bossy, sometimes jokester, now and again real serious. And the TV, sometimes it acted strange. . . . Roselle couldn't worry about that now. After Momma had gone to Jesus she'd have time to worry; the main thing now was just getting through the day.

It seemed funny to Roselle that a woman born in Reconstruction could be so jumpy and electric wired, an old lady who had boiled cane and chopped cotton back in the old-timey, so nervous. A friend had told Roselle that some old people stopped getting enough blood to their heads, which caused their brains to shrivel down like a walnut. Roselle decided that this was definitely not happening to Momma. She was getting too much blood if anything, but it was like hers had changed, thinned down to air and fire until she was ready to go off, wild and sparking, not getting old like regular folks, not humping over, weighing down or drawing into the past, but here and now jumping.

T minus . . . .

At suppertime she was full of messages, sitting over her plate swallowing, clicking her teeth, and coming out with all kinds of stuff—Jews done shot down the Arabs, Katherine Hepburn starring, 90 percent chance to rain, Lucy done screamed at Ethel, help, get me out of this lion skin, twelve ways to build yo' body, hope the Communist don't break the new year—on and on until listening made Roselle so dizzy she'd about lose her supper. She gave up trying; if Momma was going to babble like a little child, she'd treat her like one.

"White suit jump / Crack yo' skin / Get offen that bomb / All of you men."

Roselle found her way into the kitchen, opened the refrigerator, and got out a pop to settle her stomach. Damping a towel with warm water and holding it against her left ear, she sat down at the kitchen table. Momma kept up jabbering in the living room. Roselle thought about Olin asleep in there instead of being at work. He got off one or two afternoons every week, but it never ceased to worry her when she came home before 5 P.M. and found him there. Two of them laying off on the same day worried her double. She shut her left eye and squeezed the warm towel against her numb head.

Skeeeeerakkk!

Oh Lord. A terrible noise. Sounded like something great big had broke. Roselle pushed back her chair and stood up—kind of wobbly. What was that noise? She hoped Momma hadn't fell over the coffee table and died. At the living-room door, she saw Olin sitting upright on the couch, his brown working hat on the floor. He was rubbing his eyes and trying to speak.

Roselle smelled it before she saw it, even through her headache and pill-clogged head, smelled what was almost but not quite like burning rubber, what smelled a little more like the semitractortruck accident that had occurred back in 1955 down the road from her old house in Hiram, Mississippi—a jackknifed truck blowing up what the paper later called "$50,000 worth of cosmetics, skin conditioners, and ladies apparel," raining perfume, moisture cream, witch hazel, eyeliner, blush powder and deodorant, some intact in bottles and cartons, all over a cluster of sharecroppers' houses—a thundering orange mushroom that knocked out every window in sight and blanketed the neighborhood with these gifts, all the pretty fixings, sweet smellings, stockings, panties, and girdles that the ladies could ever use: sweet but kind of stinking, too, like the smell of a bus stop, a public bathroom just disinfected, or a little—just a little—like the emergency room at the colored hospital in Hiram. Now smelling that same odor, Roselle was not surprised to see something bad had happened. A big white thing was sitting on the floor, strapped down to a chair, with tubes and wires straggling back through the TV screen—or what used to be the screen and was now a jagged hole with a curl of white smoke rising out of it to the ceiling.

"Look what I done," said Momma, real weak.

Roselle looked at Momma. She was squeezed down in the chair with her hands over her face, peeking out through her fingers. For a moment the room was real quiet. Roselle said, "What *have* you done?"

Momma clicked her teeth and whimpered, "Done busted my story gettin' shed of them moonmens."

Roselle looked at the white thing. While the room remained silent, she could hope this was just a quick nightmare she was dozing into back at the kitchen table, but noises had started up that didn't sound like dreams. One side of the room was mumbling letters and numbers, and the other was clucking like a blue jay. The blue jay was Olin—his throat muscling up and down, bulging, not speaking words but just clucking and popping like an old dumb momma jay in spring—a sound he made only when he got outright wild, like the Saturday night back in Mississippi when he drank thirty-three cans of malt liquor at the Moonlight Beer & Ribs Inn and cut up so, until the owner Willy Peters chased him down and struck him up side of the head with a plumber's snake.

The numbers were coming out of the white thing, from the pipes and tubes that hung off of him, and the awful part was that Roselle could hear everything he said; it wasn't no dreamy soup of numbers like would come from a nightmare goblin moaning what sounded like arithmetic but real numbers and letters—oh Lord!

Now slowing down and saying words, too, the voice shook out of a smoking pipeline and faucets on the chest of the suit: "... X–13, X–13, X–13, PLSS is zero, X–13, X–13 + 1, X–13 + 2, X–13 + 3, X–13 + 4.... MC, do you read, do you read? I seem to have reached constant, but it is definitely X–13, do you read? X–13 + approximately 12 and running, no change, I should be amputated, do you read?"

Momma widened her fingers and looked through at the moonman. "You the stinkinest ol' tire I ever smell. What'd you bust my story fo'?"

Still clucking, Olin left the room and returned with Roselle's rolling pin. She grabbed him by the shirt. "Keep back, Olin, I think this thing come from the gov'ment. Momma, did you conjure this? If you did, put it back."

"I ain't have no truck with that ol' stinky moonman," Momma said peevishly, hunkered down in her chair, " 'cept to get him outen my TV. He can put his own self back. Bust my picture like that. . . . Now I got to 'magine my story."

Olin pulled away from Roselle and crowed out like he had just heard a good joke. "Wha! Wha!"

"What's so funny?"

"I done had these dreams," he chuckled, "had them befo', and there wasn't nothing better after I calculate how to get through them is do whatever come up. Good dream's mo' fun than six quarts of beer and honky-tonk pussy."

"Olin!" Roselle was shocked at him talking like that in front of Momma. He was generally a housebroke man.

"In good dreams, you can do just as fancy as rich folks. Hmmm. Now what is that white monstah in the floor? That a moonman?"

"Whatever it is, it belong to the U.S. gov'ment. You see the flag on its arm. We got to be careful, Olin. Sheriff put us in the jailhouse and throw away the key. You listen to me now, I got a turrible headache."

"Well well, let me check this monstah out—look about like a Ku Klux in all that white. I might just have to tap some sense into his head." Olin stalked around the white thing but kept his distance.

"Leave him alone with that rollin' pin!" Lord, Olin was acting like a sixteen-year-old stud instead of what he was.

He stood next to the moonman and cocked his ear. "Listen . . . ."

"Readout symptoms, X–13 . . . I don't know . . . thirty or forty. Heartbeat regular but fast. Perspiration. AC unit not working. Auto belts secure. Amputate, repeat, amputate. Field of vision . . . MC, you won't believe this . . . three negroid creatures in immediate field, two female, one male . . . with a clublike object. Obviously a paranoid blackout, huh-huh! Yes. Other symptoms: I cannot see, uh, the instruments. I seem to be in a large room with these three negroid . . . hallucinations. . . . MC, request information, did we launch? This is a G-black, right? MC, do you read? What is this place? Where am I?"

Olin took the moonman's severed pipe and spoke into it. "You on the outskirt of Little Rock."

". . . MC, put on the chief psychiatrist. Request aid immediately. One of these things just spoke to me."

Olin walked jauntily around the moonman, inspecting him. "Yes suh, you is just 'bout the brightest, stinkinest, most livliest dream I done had since Mona Jean Kalo. I wonder if I was to tap you on the head, you'd change to Mona Jean? She had a thang 'bout the size of a washtub. You could get in that sucker and *dance!*"

"Olin! Don't you speak of Mona Jean Kalo in my livin' room. That bitch look like a highway accident. What do you mean talkin' like that in my livin' room?"

Olin waved her off. "Hush. You won't 'member nothin' when I wakes up anyhow. Let me play with this monstah. Maybe I can get him to 'mogrify." Olin reached down with the rolling pin and tickled under the moonman's helmet.

"Sir, chief psychiatrist? Are you there? I do not read . . . maybe we have a one-way. . . . Alternatives, yes, okay. Now I want everybody at MC—and all over America—and, uh, down through history—to understand that this is impossible, totally, but the negroid male hallucination is making . . . oh no. Oh. Request instructions. What do I do? Sir, help, he is dancing suggestively in front of me! This is no G-blackout!"

Olin hummed to himself and danced like the country-boy zoot he had been twenty years ago. Despite the strange circumstances, Roselle kind of admired the way he still got around. "Yes suh," he said, "I done learn that dream time is my time. Olin is king when it come to sawin' logs. Mmmm-mmmm. . . . I mops the flo' in daylight, but night come and I is a *back do' man*."

"Olin, did you mess with Mona Jean Kalo?"

"Honey, this time of night I mess with heifers and mules. Now quit actin' so realistic. Mmmm-mmm." Olin danced around with the rolling pin.

"I is realistic. I is Roselle Smith, yo' wife."

Momma got up from her chair. "You peoples is crazy. We must get this moonman back where he belong so my TV heal up. Roberta is in the courthouse right now finding out which of them mens she married to, and I got to tune in. That wicked hussy sec'tary will be makin' up to Mr. Jim at the hospital—been doin' it three weeks straight. You wouldn't believe the mess these rich white folks get into. Why, they needs my help." Momma approached the moonman and touched him on the shoulder.

"*Aiiii!* MC, psychiatry, help! The female is touching me. I confess! I admit it! I did experiment with . . . but that was before training. My secretary influenced me. It was a small dosage, not narcotic . . . ."

"Not habit formin'," picked up Momma, "and what's better than a good night's sleep."

Olin snapped his fingers lightly, swaying to an imagined tune. "You can say that again, you old hag. You makes mo' sense in my dream than in real life. What you doin'?"

"Unh, unh! Pushin' this thing back to the TV, befo' it's too late. Hep me."

Olin stopped dancing and stood with the rolling pin at his side. "What if I was to crack that sucker? Reckon he'd turn into a big old throbbin' thang like Mona Jean?" Olin sounded a little uncertain now, like something was bothering him. Momma was pushing, tipping the moonman over backwards.

"They're attacking me," the moonman said. "Do you read? I only experimented twice. Pro-football players influenced me. Suzanne betrayed me. In Dallas. But I never did again. Honest, sir. I deserve this—whatever happens, I deserve it. Oh God. This may sound far fetched, but these creatures are real—perhaps extraterrestrial—yes. You've heard of unexplained gaseous clouds in the upper stratosphere. Psych-prep demo'ed acrophobic illusions, but these things are touching me, they are manipulating my chair. I must unbuckle and defend myself!" The moonman struggled to release himself from the tangle of straps.

Olin moved back a step. "Wait a minute heah. There's something fishy 'bout this devil. I's had lots of dreams, had enough so I couldn't tell them all if I was to sit down and talk myself into grey hair, but I ain't never had one that *stink* like this."

Roselle said, "Smell like the perfume truck that blowed up outside Hiram back in the fifties."

Olin looked up blankly. "Who you?"

"I is Roselle yo' wife, you idiot—pay mind to me! We got to help this man, not mess him up worse."

"You is Roselle my wife, huh?" He thought a while. "Sho you ain't no dream? You done rose up and act a hindrance in my dream befo'—how do I know this ain't the same?"

The moonman had gotten loose from his chest straps and was fending Momma off with karate blocks. "Sir, request hookup with Project Head. This is important. This is mortal combat. Oh speak to me Wernher—radio—someone!"

Olin picked up his hat and inspected it. "That's a awful realistic hat . . . look just like the one I works in." Thoughtfully, he put it on. "Okay, Roselle, so you is the real thang. Then what is that monstah?" He pointed at the moonman.

"That's a United State moonman. I done told you six times. Now help me."

"Hep you what?"

"Help . . . help me . . . ." Roselle's shoulders raised. "Get him out of here. Out of this house. We got enough trouble without the sheriff comin'."

Olin looked at the man, who was now working to get loose from his leg straps. Olin rubbed his chin. "Momma been tryin' to put him back in the TV. That what we oughta do? I ain't studyin' this dream no mo'. It ain't worth a shit. I do better on a nap than this." Disgruntled, Olin reached below the moonman's feet and started to tip him over.

Tottering backwards, a little puff of smoke rising from under his chair, the moonman quit struggling with his leg straps and held both hands up—stubby white gloves saying hold it. "Gosh darn it, you people listen to me!" Olin's grasp on the chair slipped, and he sat down with a thump on the living-room floor. "Now. You nice . . . people, listen here to me. I am going to cooperate. Let me ask you . . . to cooperate with me. 10–4? Let us all cooperate together. Yes, in the spirit of harmony, let us work together. . . ." The voice lowered, became confidential, a canned, tinny sound emerging from the spigots and tubes like old radio voices Roselle had heard back in the thirties. "A–2 alternative, the best considering

56

the status of my . . . status. In lieu of immediate relief, do not exacerbate nervous state by violent resistance. Such resistance involves the subject in spiralling *aphasia abasia.* Which reads don't fight it, according to Suzanne, who has a master's in English and ought to know—heh–heh. 10–4. Do you hear that, Wernher, I remember: there are always alternatives. . . . Oh but Suzanne, why did you involve me with those degenerated athletes? And then running off with a tackle. Darn it, how could you forsake an astronaut for a tackle? I should've known better than to trust you. You're just like all secretaries. . . ." The moonman choked, coughed, and a last puff of white smoke emerged from his tube.

"Wait a minute," said Momma. "Sec'tary name of Suzanne done got you in trouble, you say? Wait one minute. Oh Lawd, I see now. Po' thing! I should have knowed. You done bust through so Momma could hep you. Oh child, I'm happy you did. Roselle, quick, we got to minister to Jim, get him some ice tea."

Roselle's head was getting heavy from the medicine, and she couldn't see straight. Her stomach felt like a boiling cauldron, and her brain like it was packed with big cotton wads. She did what Momma said—went to the kitchen and made a glass of iced tea with two teaspoons of sugar and a squirt of lemon. Back in the living room, Momma was giggling and carrying on, talking like an old friend to the moonman, who nodded his big white canister and agreed right along with her. But when she asked him to take off his helmet, he got jumpy and started to fend her off again.

"Well, how will you drink yo' tea?"

"Oh, I'll just . . . hold it. Yes, it will be very nice to hold it."

"Jim, you don't hold ice tea, you drinks it. That sec'tary done give you nervous tension. And her readin' the Scripture! You should see the look on her face when you goes to sleep. So many times I wanted to tell you—I just hurt inside I wanted to tell so much: that sec'tary is a *hussy.*"

"Yes," the helmet nodded slowly. "She is. I learned my lesson. I'll never again gamble my career for such a—hussy."

Momma fluttered at his agreement. "Now I do understand it was a blow to hear yo' wife is married to fo' mens, but you know that wasn't her fault."

"Four men? Yes, oh yes indeed, four—at least."

"Child, there is plenty of womens that marry three, fo' mens and *ain't* crazy. You, who has suffered so much—po' Jim—you know that's the way the world turn. Here, let me unfasten this old stupid thing so you can drink yo' tea, which is fresher than fresh perked.

"No! Do not approach my suit. Do not make any alteration whatsoever. Never tamper with life support. I'm not resisting, you understand, but life support is essential in this environment. I will cooperate, but there are limits."

Momma hovered over him with the glass of tea. "I know what we'll do. Olin, hold up this tube, and I'll pour Jim's tea in that-away. In General Hospital they use these here tubes to feed folks that's real beat up, whose teeth done fell out or somethin', or got their brains squashed and all such stuff and ain't got 'nuf sense to swallow. It happen mo' than you think. One man, he got knocked in the head with a ax and his stomach cease to grind. Nothin' else wrong, just his stomach stop, and the doctor couldn't get it to commence. Po' man need some Rolaids. He died, too, and they cut him open and found a brick down there. Me, I got five proud teeth and could chew a tin can if I please. Hold up this tube, Olin."

Grumbling, Olin held up the tube, and Momma poured in the tea, lemon and all, without spilling a drop. The moonman began to thrash around in his chair. "Help! They have poured ice tea into my britches, er, life-support system. I tell you, these things are real!"

Olin snorted and turned away. "This damn dream make me sick. I'm gonna take a nap." He fell onto the couch, bumping his head against Roselle's thigh, and started snoring like a train. Roselle poked his ribs. "Unh!" Eyelids fluttered.

"Olin, you done took some of Momma's nerve pills, didn't you?"

"Mmmm...."

"Nerve pills!"

"Mmm–huh . . . feel pretty good till I had this jangly old . . . ."
He fell off snoring again just like that.

Roselle sighed. "Well, that makes three of us. Maybe we in
hell. All these years I thought I was going to the other place." She
blinked through the fuzz—a growing weight behind her forehead
and eyes, so heavy that it felt like any minute her head would roll
off and crash to the floor, maybe fall right on through, forehead
and eyes first, splintering hardwood and mashing like a cannonball
into the dirt beneath the house. Momma and the moonman seemed
to be getting along good now, having a regular social: him bowing
and nodding from his chair real gentlemanly, agreeing with her—
except for his puffy white suit with knobs, straps and tubes, acting
like the minister on Sunday visit, while she spoke of how sweet he
was to finally come see her and how she done watched him through
the years, so many times wanting to admonish him of evil that was
being worked. She apologized if he had got the wind knocked out
busting loose from the TV like that.

The canister mumbled, "No problem. I am trained . . . ."

Momma took a drink of tea. "What done it was a riddle I learn
back in the old days."

"Oh—how is that?" the moonman asked.

Momma lifted her eyebrows. "Old fat slave witch from Mis-
s'sippi told me 'bout a hundred years ago. Lulu they call her, she
live out in the woods and trade in fortune and greegree, sold a good
enough sight of it that she hire childrens to hunt moss and beetles
and such stuff. Had a regular factory out in the swamp a'makin'
these charms and hex, sellin' them to folks. If you was to pay her
high enough, she'd give you full-circle protection."

"This riddle, you say, is what gave me . . . brought me here?"

" 'Less you brought yo'self. Lulu, she had a crystal ball that
some would ride a hundred miles to gaze into—I'm talkin' about
white folks now. She say it come offen the King of France breakfast
table, where he use it to keep a lookout on his empire, so it have
all the practice in the world, she claim, spyin' out the mos' impor-

tant thing to come up next. This one I just use come outen Lulu's ball, he–he!" Momma leaned back and clapped her hands. "She give it to me one afternoon when I brung her a white angel what I done happen onto down the woods 'tween the gin and my house. I knowed Lulu could use it, you see. It was a *big* mushroom—I'd say more than a foot, up above two, maybe three to five foot tall, and I had to use Daddy's wheelbarrow to carry it. 'Sides, if you was to touch a white angel, you'd go up in smoke. They is poison and rise up overnight in the darkest place of the wood, grow with white wings—dark, child, all around, but themself so white that it shock yo' eyes to come onto them. I shovel it into the wheelbarrow and roll it up to Lulu's door and call out, and when she hear I done brung her a white angel, she begin to throw a hex on the spot, through the do'. She come out directly, puttin' down the grumblinest, ugliest, powerfullest hex I done heard to this day, and next thing you know she had done busted that mushroom down to little chunks and throwed it into a pot of magic oil that was cooking in the yard. She'd bottle this oil, you see, and sell it fo' two bits a lick: cure what ails—artheritus, headache, boils, lumbago, canker sore, whoopin' cough, slow fever—you name it and Lulu show you where to rub on this oil for relief—ague, bruise, perspiration stain, scalds, dog bite, catarrh, scabies, irregularity, milk crust, mornin' backache, swelled joint, problem dandruff—this stuff fix just 'bout anything."

"This is very informative, but could we, uh, get on with this riddle. I want to cooperate . . . ."

Momma's pinpoint eyes blinked, a look of sad love melting her face, softening the withered tightness of her skin.

Bone heavy, headache muffled in thickening waves of medicine, Roselle remembered that look on Momma's face from way back, thirty years ago and more, from as far back as she could remember. Feet and ankles numb, electric fingers playing over them, Roselle's body climbed with sleep; words angled sideways and were sucked into the weight behind her eyes. The room flickered with silver light. Floating now, spread out and waving like riverweeds in a muddy current, Roselle appeared, softly, and disappeared, reaching upward not quite to the surface, sinking, dragged, and rolling in the darkness. She seemed to be stopping, shutting down, her body itself a fluid going down the drain.

Momma's face shone with that sweet look, that old tenderness Roselle hadn't seen in such a long time. "After comin' all this way, sholy you'll take off that hat and let me see yo' face. Just one minute. Momma won't hold you back. You can go on to the hospital after . . . ."

The moonman groaned and began tearing at his straps, kicking his legs, crawling off the chair headfirst into the TV. "MC, help. This negroid is threatening to remove my helmet. Whenever I cooperate, they threaten me. Help." He tried to push through the broken screen but couldn't get past his helmet. "I am cooperating fully. Not resisting. Do anything you want, just get me back to the vehicle. 10–4?" The moonman sounded pitiful and weak, like he had given up.

Momma sighed. "All right, child. Get ready and I send you back in the hospital." She cranked her arm around.

"No, not the hospital—the vehicle. I'm going to the *moon*." He writhed and pushed, trying to get into the TV.

"Moon? Moon?" Momma whirled her arm around faster, working up to lay a hex. She screeched like some awful old witch. "I thought you's goin' to the hospital!"

"No, the moon!"

"Momma gonna put you in the hospital."

"No, put me anywhere, but not the hospital!"

"Whee! Whee! Power's boilin'. To the hospital. Lawd! It's comin'. Whee! Momma fired up. Get ready." Her arm rotating around like a windmill, Momma spoke words that didn't make any sense to Roselle—just a bunch of sad sounds clanking against each other like boxcars down a track. Roselle wanted to understand what Momma said, what she now wound up and croaked out, loosed from her spindly throat like stones—but she slipped and was blank.

. . . And then through her drowse heard snoring and moans of deep misery. As she poured out of herself, gathered in thickness and poured out and down, a voice: "Has I got the ambulance or not? ... Yes suh, on the outskirt. . . . Oh no suh, this is a white man—in an expensive suit. I done tried to hex him to the hospital, but he want to get on this heah kerosene rocket ship and fly to the moon so bad he done jam my greegree. I know it *seem* ridiculous, but afta' all the po' thing been in the hospital so long he be confused. Now he done stuck his head in the TV and won't come out, groanin' something fierce, and tell the truth, suh, I is worried. Be certain with Certs. He done already had two heart-attack breakdowns when his wife got around with three other mens in her sleep, so to speak. . . . No. Oh no suh, I ain't drunk. An old thing like me get drunk and I'd go crazy. One thing—is yo' ambulance ride on steel-belt radios?"

5

FROG GIG

FIVE hours ago Annie and I walked through an air-conditioned tube onto a jet in San Francisco. Now, at dusk, I sit alone in the field behind her house, admiring a saw-briar nip on my left ankle, chewing the Dr. Pepper sap out of a sassafras twig, the smell of wild mint from plants squashed under me like cool air loosening the July Arkansas heat that clings to my skin—remembered heat, but even closer in dusk than I had remembered. I spit out the sassafras and remember more, remember to get myself here again. Only four years away from Arkansas—I grew up in a larger town, one hundred-forty miles from here—and the heat quickens my memory, but there are four years of hair springing from my skull. Laying down Annie's daddy's twenty gauge, which he asked me to carry in hopes I might stumble on the rabbit that's been plundering his garden, I look around: a plum thicket behind me, blackberries within reaching distance, and a scrawny persimmon tree between me and the last light in the sky. I pick a handful of blackberries—furry in my palm and—sour.

Thinking about walking across the pasture to Johnny Irwin's house: my oldest friend in Parson—Johnny who invited me down the summer we met at Boy's State (age seventeen), promising that we would stand in the train tunnel for the Little Rock midnight special, a craze that Johnny himself had recently started, that we would go skiing behind a seventy-five horsepower Mercury and have dates with lusty women (I taught him the word "lusty," which delighted him and convinced me I was a genius). I came—long trip by myself in a white Austin Healey Sprite, stud on the highway, kind of European, metropolitan visiting the provinces (my town was sixty thousand, Parson a mere three thousand), and got there to find skiing not only behind a big motor, but skiing slalom, on trick skis, over ski jumps, through cottonmouth-infested, lily-padded shallow waters, which Johnny did standing on his hands in a red saucer, his feet in the air, laughing like a lunatic, and us going to the tunnel—constructed in 1900, the year of Annie's father's birth, by convicts, seventeen of whom died in an explosion—sure enough at midnight with a half dozen other beer-befuddled kids, standing inside, holding onto jagged rock walls so the towering blur of that highball roar would not hypnotize us and draw us under its wheels, and a date the next night with Lawanda Griggs, taking Johnny's Ford, while he and Mary Bender took the Sprite, because he wanted speed in order to race the midnight special from Old Wire Road to the tunnel, and I wanted space in which Lawanda and I could be comfortable at the drive-in, which worked out pretty well, as Lawanda loved Johnny's radio, which had the first echoing rear speaker in Parson, and Mary was snowed out of her mind by that little bug convertible, teensy as a go-cart and with seat belts that they strapped tight when the train came around the bend, which must have been just about the time Lawanda turned off the sound of *Shark Man at Bikini Beach* and turned on the radio, KROC, Little Rock, playing "Sugar Shack" several times an hour that night, soft and tricky: *There's a crazy little place across the track*— while Shark Man stalked silently screaming pneumatic blondes across Bikini Beach—*and everybody calls it the sugar shack*—and Lawanda turned to me, altogether unexpectedly, and grabbed my ear, saying, "you ever git anybody to tongue it," while Johnny and Mary barreled down Old Wire Road, beating the train to the crossing by several seconds and came to a gravel-exploding stop two miles farther at the place above the tunnel, as Lawanda stuck her hot huge tongue in my ear and simultaneously caressed my already tumescent blue jeans and *across the track*, while Johnny pulled Mary down the hill, pushed her into the humming mouth of the

64

tunnel, back against the wet rock wall, *and everybody calls it the sugar shack*, and I, overwhelmed, returned the compliment in Lawanda's ear as she unzipped my pants and the midnight special, and I withdrew my tongue, squirmed sideways, seeing Shark Man dismembering a roomful of blondes, blasted through the opening, as I tried to keep from going off too early, like a giant steel fist, as Lawanda was just getting it out, and Mary screamed noiselessly in the roar *and Everybody Calls it the Sugar Shack.*

I came back to Parson every chance I got. Johnny and I fished, skied, and hunted; one night we camped on the Cadro, Parson's water supply, a thick brown stream that creeps like a dying snake through the bottoms, smelling like mud, gar carcasses, cow piss, and unknown other things, altogether like an unimaginably evil growth—mold on the eye of a well-fermented murderer's corpse—camped there in order that we might see the mystery light, which sometimes (in the dark of the moon, according to the legend) appears under Highway 9 bridge; we missed it, perhaps because we got slobbering drunk on Yucca Flats (maraschino cherries, heaps of sugar, and a fifth of cheap vodka) and fell asleep earlier than expected; I had dates with Lawanda, Johnny with cheerleaders, and we drove to Pillar, ten miles south on a dirt road, to the Imperial Rib House—an old flatboard shack, low ceiling and sagging floor, like a ghost heap in moonlight, inside bathed in the soft gaudy lambency of a dozen beer advertisements—serving what must have been the best ribs and hottest sauce in all of southeastern Arkansas. Always drunk—Johnny not used to it, a bad drunk, and I proud to lead him into debauchery, to bring a touch of urban nihilism into his simple world, but afraid that his Church of Christ parents would disapprove and ban me from visiting—which they never did, because, as I learned, they never banned anything Johnny did, at least not out loud, since boys would be boys, even devils sometimes, and besides it was kind of entertaining to hear him talk about it—saucering on his head over water moccasins, standing in the tunnel when the train went through—his mother clucking, "You're gonna get squashed, boy," and father scratching his paw, drinking a coke, muttering, "Anybody'd stand in that tunnel at midnight deserves to get squashed."

We usually had to go to church on Sunday, but other than that there were no restrictions. One weekend when his folks were out of town, we drank Yucca Flats for two days, until Johnny went crazy and tried to cook a two-pound "hamburger steak" by globbing it around a broom handle and holding it over the stove; it naturally didn't work—dropped into the fire, onto the floor, causing Johnny to fall into a deep and geunine despair that ended with his falling asleep on the toilet and spending the night with his head in the shower and legs on the bathroom rug. I awakened Sunday afternoon to find the cow, neglected two mornings, on the front porch mooing the most mournful moo I had ever heard—her lugubrious rebuke being the only I ever received in Parson—a town that was by then, for all time, my wilderness, my region of lawlessness, where the only reputation to worry about was Johnny's, and where there was not even the good influence of true love to keep me in line, as Annie Cain, living just across the pasture, managed to elude me until college, where I was surprised to meet a new girl from Sodom and Gomorrah. She carried, I will not deny, a nimbus of Parson about her, or so I imagined, and we fell in love in one week.

After picking another few blackberries, I head back, sleepy, to her—and tomorrow I'll see Johnny. It's too dark to be out here barefoot.

*   *   *

The next morning I call Johnny's house and find that he is working as assistant druggist at Tubman's to fulfill a pharmacy school requirement. He beams out like a lighthouse when I walk in, my shagginess apparently no surprise, not even tempering his warmth under the bifocal glances of Mr. Tubman behind the counter. Outside, he makes a friendly jab or two—you can take off your wig now—and I jab back with the expected: What's the matter, you afraid you'll lose your job? He says hell no, Tubman isn't paying

him a cent anyway, this is "for the experience"; he'd bring an orang-
utan in there if he wanted to and Tubman couldn't say much. He
tells me that pharmacy school grew some marijuana for experi-
ments, and he'd have stolen some sure as hell, if they hadn't hired
two cops to guard it at night when it was harvest tall. Did I have
some? We should go frog gigging tonight—have to borrow Mr.
Cain's outboard since he'd just about worn out Mr. Wendell's,
borrowing it all the time; tell him we're going to Uncle Dwain's
out by the ferry and be ready at 8:30. Wait, you have to see my
pillow. Pillow? Yeah, I brought it down here to show some people.
He goes inside and returns with a red furry pillow with four ap-
pendages dangling from it—got him with a .22 pistol when I was
checking trotlines on the Cadro last week—a fox—didn't see him
but could see his eyes, one shot right in the nose, Mary stole the
skin when it wasn't even hardly dried and sewed it up into a pillow,
trying to hint that I stay home a little instead of going out hunting
all the time—isn't it ridiculous? And speaking of that, do you want
to be best man two weeks from now: We're finally taking the fatal
step.

Supper that night at the Cain's is catfish, fried okra, corn on
the cob, pole beans, tomatoes, biscuits, blackberry cobbler, and
iced tea. Mrs. Cain (age sixty-eight, mother of seven), who has
been sewing with Annie this afternoon, conjures it in about a half
hour, banging doors, clanking pots, and stomping around as if she
were mad, but more likely because she has cooked enough meals in
this kitchen to have lost all sentimentality over it, to have long
since broken what was breakable and gotten used to everything
else, handling her pots and skillets as though they were parts merely
of herself, not to be coddled or lingered over. It is the only thing
she is noisy at. The rest of the time she is as light, as unobtrusive as
a girl out of old-fashioned finishing school (although she never got
near one), but solid, walking like an Indian with each foot in front
of itself, and very still when she stands or sits.

Over cobbler, Mr. Cain tells me where I can find an extra
shear pin for the motor. That's okay, I tell him, we'll be careful not

to hit any snags. Later, in our room, Annie says I should have accepted.

"He wouldn't have offered if he didn't want you to take it. Go on now and get one. He's had that motor ever since before I can remember, and if anything happens to it you might as well just stay in the swamp till it's fixed. Now go get a shear pin."

"Quit ordering me around, woman—and quit talking like a country hick," I grab her by the waist and flash my eyes like William Buckley at her. "You saond lak a by gawd cull."

"Go get a shear pin."

"I wuz jist a'fixin to roll me up a joint!"

"Not so loud. What do you want a joint for?"

"Johnny wants to try it out."

"Then you better take two shear pins—and a paddle. You'll be running over logs and stumps and probably alligators before the night's up."

"Alligators!"

"All I'm saying is take good care of that motor. If Daddy lost it he'd have to go without."

I release her. "Next I'll be putting up collateral. I'd just as soon paddle."

"Okay . . . I'm sorry. But you have to take care of things, that's all—down here you have to."

I am digging in the suitcase for the medicine bottle of grass that I think we brought. "Do you remember Lawanda Griggs?"

"Why—you and Johnny going out to get you a little tonight?"

"Oink, oink."

She plops down on the bed. "All I remember about Lawanda is passing her in the halls. She was pale as chalk all the time and held her nose high—I guess because it was kind of Roman looking."

"Did I ever tell you about the time I hypnotized her?"

"No. I don't want you to, either. Go get a shear pin."

At 9 P.M., just dark, Johnny and I bomb down Old Wire Road in the Green Goose, the '51 Chevrolet pickup he's had since he was eleven, out of hills and into bottoms, between fields planted

68

in cotton and soybeans. The Goose is coming apart at the seams, just like it was four years ago, and I have to sit with my legs crossed in the seat, holding the door, which rattles with an inch play, with one hand and the back of the seat with the other, to keep from falling through the floorboard, which doesn't exist.

"I didn't tell you the exact truth about where we're going. I said Uncle Dwain's—well we might go there too—but first I want to check out the shit pond. I don't think it'll hurt the motor; there been people in there with outboards, I'm sure of it."

"What's the shit pond?"

"That's just what it is. Parson pumps sewage out there to settle."

"Sewage? You mean real sewage? We're going floating around in sewage?"

"That's right. We're going to get right down to the hard-core stuff, Alder. More frogs out there than you can shake a stick at."

"And you're going to eat these frogs? You're crazy."

"It won't hurt you long as you don't gig them—some kind of poison might fester in the stab holes. You got to catch them with your hands."

"What about the motor? It's water cooled, liable to jam up. I don't think we better do it."

"No, I never saw any turds or anything in there. They ground all that up and put chemicals, disinfectants, in there."

"So you're gonna eat frogs that have been drinking ground-up chemically disinfected shit water."

"We've done it before; sweetest frog we ever ate—ask Mary. Long as he's healthy he's okay, and you clean him real good."

I argue against it, but Johnny just laughs at me as if I were trying to be funny, which causes me to want to be funny—an old pattern with us—and pretty soon he's speaking of the shit pond with such favor that you'd think it was a health spa, a virtual Hot Springs, and I'm saying I don't want to die an ignominious death, which is the funniest thing he's ever heard, and then we're unloading the boat, scratching it across the top of a barbed-wire fence and down the evenly sloping bank of the pond, still arguing, and I'm expecting to be overcome at any moment by a foul odor, to be asphyxiated on the spot—but now at the water's edge, we set the boat down, and there is no smell, as Johnny goes back for the batteries and lamp. Silence. Not a ripple or a sound, not even crickets. Clouds are blowing fast across a slice of moon, and it seems funny that down here it is so still. As my eyes adjust to darkness, the pond begins to take on vague dimensions, a square perhaps two hundred yards to a side; there is a concrete building nearby, probably the turd grinder and disinfectant injector, but making no sound, and I'm wishing Johnny would hurry up and get back here with the light. A slight breeze across the pond, and I sniff suspiciously—absolutely dead nothing—so perhaps the disinfectant really works, unless the stench is so incredible that it transcends the range of the nose, as a dog whistle does the ear, or bludgeons the olfactory sensors into shock and coma. I feel my nose to make sure it's okay.

Johnny is back with the lamp, a portable sealed beam powered by dry-cell batteries a friend borrowed from the telephone company. "Let's get going Alder, in the boat. I'll shove us off."

"All right, but if I fall into that pond, you better just gig me between the eyes and let me sink."

The boat slides unctuously into the pond, and he plugs in the light, which aims for a moment directly into the water, unable despite arc-white brightness to penetrate beyond a few inches. It is some shade of green: opaque, thick brownish green, like motor oil, and it doesn't splash when the boat rocks, as if too thick. The outboard is cranky, and I imagine the worst—that it is already stopped up with slime. Johnny is no help, languidly dangling a paddle in the water—"Looks like asparagus soup." It finally starts, and soon we're trolling near the bank, which he scans with the light, immediately attracting a haze of bugs. I am instructed in the art of frog-gig trolling, as we slide through the shit pond, Mr. Cain's motor now purring like a well-fed cat. The bugs get worse, clouding furious in the burst of light that Johnny holds at arm's length, above his head. They are in my ears and nostrils and everywhere touching my skin, but touching softly and making no sound at all, even as the cloud becomes a typhoon, a silent maelstrom of flying bugs spiralling upward as if to carry the boat off the water.

"What are they?"

"I don't know . . . sewer skeeters maybe . . . look, over there, I see one."

"See what? I can't see my hand in front of my face."

"Take us in."

I aim in the general direction of the shore, fanning my face to keep from suffocating on sewer skeeters, Johnny tells me to cut the motor, and before I can, he's hauling out a three-foot moccasin gigged in two places, writhing on the forks and striking numbly at the wood, pulling it to the side of the boat and slicing its neck with a hunting knife. The mouth, even as the head dangles half severed, opens slowly, exposing pure white.

"Look at that sucker." He scrapes the snake loose, and it plops into the heavy water, sinking.

A moment passes, and I am suddenly aware that the water into which I am staring is no longer the violently dead green reflected in Johnny's lamp but sunk into blackness, as he scans the shore ahead, and I say: "You see any more frogs, John?"

"No, but I smell a few snakes."

"I thought we were after frogs."

"What?" He turns the light into my face.

"To eat."

"They won't eat you. I gig them tight before I bring them out."

Blinded, I say nothing. He pushes us away from the bank, and the boat catches on something. I fumble with the motor, suddenly weak in my shoulders and arms, again aware of the swarm of bugs. "Better not kill any more snakes; they control these sewer skeeters."

"That right? They aren't doing a very good job."

"That's because there aren't enough snakes."

"Always enough snakes; you don't have to worry about that. Besides, the frogs eat the sewer skeeters, not the snakes. The snakes eat the frogs. I haven't seen a frog yet, but I've already seen three snakes and nine zillion sewer skeeters, which means we're doing right by this pond to kill a few moccasins. Just like killing gar: you don't and there won't be anything but gar."

I mull over that one a while. Johnny isn't usually that logical. Maybe pharmacy school is a logical place. Or maybe he's been thinking in advance. I'm still fumbling with the rope, which won't pull. "I don't think that's why you're pronging these snakes, Johnny; you just like to prong them, don't you?"

"Sure." He puts down the light, illuminating his chin and eyebrows from below, and takes off his sweater. "I like it. I wouldn't be out here floating around in the scum if I didn't." His face looks wider, heavier than it was four years ago—a trick of the light.

"The rope won't pull. It's stuck."

"Stuck?"

"Tight. I can't pull it."

"Prop must be wound around a big old green one—you reckon?"

I try to pull up the motor, but the whole thing is stuck, and the boat dips as I try to muscle it loose. "Something's holding it down."

Johnny and I switch places, and he tries to get it loose. We decide the prop must be stuck in roots. "That's the damndest thing I ever saw. We're going to have to get at it with a knife, Alder."

"You mean under the water?"

"Yeah, chop it loose."

"How do you know it's not a big moccasin down there tangled up in the prop?"

"That'd be a bitch, wouldn't it?" He aims the light into the murk and pokes around with the gig. "Yeah, it's roots all right. You got a pocketknife?"

". . . Yeah, here you go."

"Why don't you cut that sucker loose."

"Me? You're the one by the motor. I can't reach that far."

"I don't want to stick my hand down in that stuff, Alder. Might eat my arm off."

"Why I thought you liked this pond, Johnny."

"I love it. I just can't stand to touch it. I'll flip you for it."

I get out a coin, fighting a sense of doom; I never win a fifty-fifty when I'm scared of losing. Tails, sure enough, and now I have to prepare myself, to roll up my sleeve for a few minutes, as long as possible, a neat trick with a short-sleeve, and then, no more stalling—close my eyes and—plunge.

"Don't get your hair wet!"

"Shut up."

Grappling the prop nervously, I try not to notice the feel of the water around my fingers. The snag, something long and skinny, not roots, is caught between prop and drive shaft, strung tight, but covered by a soft and delicate scum that squishes through my fingers and tickles my wrist.

"*Gawdamn!*" My hand ejaculates from the pond.

"What's wrong?"

"Scum—some kinda gawd-awful scum."

"That's nothing but moss, Alder. It won't hurt you." He's laughing at me.

"If it's moss, it's some kind of special moss, and I don't like it." I beat my hand on the middle seat to pound off the water. "And there's something like a cable holding the prop. Some kind of steel thing. I don't like it, I tell you."

Johnny is laughing his ass off now. "A cable!"

"It's got us caught, John."

He laughs so hard he drops his light. "Sheeit Alder—don't tickle me like that. Liked to lost my light." He picks it up, flashes the shore, and suddenly the gig is in his hand stabbing the shallows, and I see a muddy tail rise slowly and brush through the grass as if trying to crawl off backwards, now stabbing again, pop of barbs through flesh, through scales and cold flesh, and I grip the steering handle, as Johnny stands, the light under his arm, and raises the gig from the water, writhing with snake—two snakes—encircling each other in tightening, loosening, tightening knots, brought closer to the boat, as one of them veers through the light, striking the

other full in the neck, once and again and mechanically again, and
I say, "Kill them."

"They're killing each other." He holds them out, winding and
unwinding, striking. "I'm afraid of those suckers. Those suckers are
pissed."

And so am I, real strangely pissed at him for killing two more
snakes while we sit here stuck by Mr. Cain's motor in the shit pond
—holding them out as they contort now languidly and bleed into
silence—and I jump half out of the damn boat when I catch my
hands, fingers, beshitted and clean, twining each other—jerk them
apart and grab both sides of the boat.

"What's wrong, a tidal wave coming?"

"No." That's all I can say. No. One stiffens, the other again,
weakly, sinking into its neck. My stomach threatening to cave in,
I look away into darkness, twisting the throttle of the dead motor
to full speed, imagining it a seventy-five instead of a three, like
Johnny's old skiing motor, and us planing out on this shit pond,
all the way across the congealing green thick surface and up the
bank, out across the pasture and through the clear night, skimming
over bean fields and through pastures of astonished Herefords,
churning circles around the midnight sleep of Parson. Johnny
maneuvers the snakes carefully toward the boat, unsheathes his
knife, hacks off their heads, then props the gig so that the snakes
dangle in the pond, stirring in the blood that runs down their
trunks in quiver and lash of death convulsion, spotlighted like some
grisly demonstration. He sheathes his knife, glancing at me. A
moment of silence, one shiny corpse still undulating in the corner
of my eye. I find myself pulling out the joint and lighting it, with
a sudden glimmer of hope, even triumph, something like Popeye
must feel each time he discovers a can of spinach, taking a good
lungful, passing it to him.

"What's that?"

"Vietnamese—the finest. Suck deep and hold it down for a
while."

"Marijuana?"

74

"Yes." He sniffs cautiously, hesitates, then takes a light puff. "It won't do you any good unless you inhale."

"I was just tasting it." He inhales, coughs. "What'll happen to me?"

"You'll turn into a pumpkin."

"Really—what'll happen?" He puffs again.

"I don't know, but one thing I'll warn you against: don't look at those snakes."

"Why?"

"Because they'll hypnotize you."

He takes several worthwhile tokes, squeezing the joint between the thumbs and forefingers of both hands, as if it were threatening to jump from his grip, holding it two feet from his face between puffs. "What do I do now?"

"Let me have some." I stoke up a bit, and the sewer skeeters lose their immediacy, become a soft moving fog, a white aureole filling the light around the snakes. Johnny takes the last few puffs, grimacing, handling the burning nub gingerly. "What I do with it now?"

"Eat it."

"You're bullshitting me. Come on now Alder, don't bullshit me—I'm getting scared."

"Here, I'll eat it."

"Don't do it."

He finally gives it to me, I drop it sizzling onto my tongue and swallow, feeling oddly like a prestidigitator on stage. "Do you remember when I hypnotized Lawanda?" He sits there with his mouth open. "Are you eating sewer skeeters or just thinking about something?" He is silent. "Johnny?"

"Where can I get me some of that stuff?"

"I'll send you some. You feel funny?"

"I ain't scared any more." He leans over and starts juggling the wires of the lamp.

"What you doing?"

"Light's low—plugging in another bladdery."

"Bladdery?"

"Blad—badderly. Shit I'm tongue-tied."

"Do you remember when I hypnotized her? It was one Christmas vacation."

"Yes I remember, you devil!" He picks up the light and blinds me. "You laid her out and held a candle on her, and that little top she was wearing would ride up showing her belly, whitest piece of meat I ever saw 'sides Mary in January, and you kept saying 'The fog is sleepy, the fog is sleepy.' "

" 'The candle is sleep' was what I said, and she went under; I did the arm-pinch check to be sure it was a deep trance. . . ."

"She didn't feel it, then you let Mary and I pinch her to prove it 100 percent—I remember that because I pinched the diddledoo out of her and she didn't even twitch. Mary got a pretty good litch in, herself—a litch—a lick, got a good lick."

"She was under. But I can't remember. . . ."

"That's when I saw what happened to her: wax dripped all over down her belly and button, and I can see it too: wax. Alder, you devil."

"Take the light out of my face, Johnny—I can't see."

"I got to keep my eye on you. My head's feeling broad. Is that normal?"

"Does it feel like a pumpkin?"

He turns the light onto his own face, staring out blindly. "Now tell me the truth, is it bigger?"

"No, but it's turning orange. You better not go home tonight or your mother'll make a pie out of you."

"Shit fire, I'm gonna dangle these snakes down your neck unless you sit bullquitting me!" He picks up the gig and levers the snakes toward me, wiggling them for semblance of life, the light cutting, lurching berserk through sewer skeeters, raw muddy-smelling meat in my face.

"No! Stop! You're not a pumpkin." I reach out to guard myself, but they move closer, Johnny laughing his old maniacal laugh

76

behind the glare, as against my elbow wet metallic skin slides, painting them with unimaginable substances, all the visceral leavings, ooze, compounds of human waste, spit blobs, dishwater, toilet-bowl cleaner, tomato soup, mouth wash, salad oil, vomitings, tooth-brushings, baby shit, Fab, Blast, spinach juice, and impacted stools; all the squirtings, sprinklings, droppings, sweatings, grindings, and gruntings of Parson, Arkansas, alchemized in chemicals and snake blood, rubbing against my bare arms and threatening my face.

"You're not a pumpkin!"

I finally grab a snake in self-defense, trying to jerk the gig from Johnny's hand. He holds tight and I hold tight, and after a pull-and-push tussle, we both give up—the light shining up from the floor between us. "Help me remember what happened that night, and you're not a pumpkin," I say, still holding the snake.

Johnny composes himself for a moment, staring intently into the lamp. "I was telling you up until you bullshitted me. We were having a party at my house, parents gone to Thorndike over night, and you got Lawanda real juiced up on Red Death or whatever it was we drank, laid her down, dripped wax onto her, and told her she was dead asleep. I started laughing at the wax on her belly, which got Mary and some of the others laughing, and you nearly did too when you saw it; then you got the idea to drip some more, only higher, to show everybody that she was into a deep one, I guess. You hitched up her blouse a little and dripped about a half cup up under her solar plexus, made a little mountain right there on her white. . . ."

"Skin."

"I can *see* it right now, Alder. You can too; what are we talking about it for? It takes me too long to figure it out."

"You're getting better. Go ahead."

"All right, then . . . well then was when Mary whispered in my ear, 'He ain't gonna *do* anything to her, is he?' and I said, 'No, except chop off her titties and cause them to grow back again,' which you heard and split up double and actually fell on the floor laughing about, and everybody else was tittling and giggling kind of nervous because half of them thought you was crazy as a coot anyway and now had just slipped on over the edge. Then you got up and saw she was still under and caused her to do all kinds of rigamarole: hold up two books with a stiff arm, lift up her leg and cause it to float through space out over the rug, and then walk into the bedroom with her eyes closed and circle the bed seventeen times, then to moan out loud like a constipated hog—that's what you said, don't look at me like that—and then you had her lie back down and stay asleep while you cussed her out."

"What!"

"You didn't say it that way, but you did it. She laid there smiling like an idiot while you cussed her—a few little ones first like 'bawdy wench'—I always did like that one—then like 'skag,' 'tail,' 'gunch' . . . I don't know . . . 'furrburger,' 'nooky'—others I can't remember—and Mary got pissed, told you to quit that because the girl couldn't defend herself; you said that's what you were proving beyond the shadow of a doubt, that she was really hypnotized. Then you decided to make her repeat words after you, to say I am a such and such; you'd say 'scunch' and she'd say, real quiet and spooky, 'I am a scunch,' 'I am a snatch,' 'I am all-around good pussy. . . .' "

" 'I am a pig.' "

"Yeah, like that, 'I am a box.' Then . . . hey Alder."

"What?"

"Why don't you let go of those snakes?"

"Finish what happened."

"I can't finish. You're making faces at me—I can't stand it—squeezing those snakes and grinding your faces around at me like a loony—quit it! Shit. Now let go of that. You trying to hypnotize me?"

"Abble dabble, I'll make you swim under water to the other bank unless you tell me the rest while I'm wound up to listen. Get it over with."

"Don't you remember by now? Quit looking at me like that. You look like a loon—hoo!" He jiggles the gig and leans forward, hoodooing me, "Hoo. Don't you like it? *Hooo!*" He stands, suddenly inspired, rocks the boat, crouching, rolling his eyes, waving the gig through billows of sewer skeeters, chanting, "And then you had her call up memories: what she did on April nineteenth two years before, what she ate for lunch on her sixth birthday, how long her first boyfriend's dong was, when she had her first filling—all sorts of deep shit. Then you sent Wilson out after some manure and held it under her nose. . . ."

"And told her it was the sweetest aroma in the world."

"You said it was more heavenly than White Shoulders perfume, which was saying pretty much, because every girl there had it on and you couldn't have smelled a fresh patty over it, much less that dry one; then you told her that after she woke up she'd climb onto a chair whenever I squeaked like a mouse, get one degree hotter every time you said the word 'sweat,' lose all control over her muscles whenever she heard 'loose,' and have such a strong hunger for dill pickles that she'd be willing to kill to get some."

"I remember. You've told me enough."

He continues, wielding the snaky gig like a wand, feinting in as if to dub me on the shoulder. "She woke up and commenced to get hot before you even said 'sweat,' stood on the chair every time she noticed me, begged us to turn on the air conditioner, fell flat as a sack of flour when you said 'loose,' and laid there sweating like a champ, moaning for dill pickles, and for us to get rid of that big mouse, which was me just squeaking now and then. She was confused, Alder, and you done it. You done it, you devil."

I slap the snakes away, remembering, "You were a pretty good mouse yourself, gave it more than a squeak if I remember right; twitched your nose, clicked your teeth, even wiggled your ears at her once, which sent her crawling into the kitchen."

"Like she couldn't decide whether she was a sack of flour or not—caught half between that and getting the hell away from the giant mouse."

"You must have looked awful."

"Then you said 'sweat' three times, sitting there with your

arms folded, looking scientific, and somebody—Mary—stood in the door and told what she did: put her wrists and face under the faucet, got two pickles out of the refrigerator, ate one and fanned herself with the other, unbottoned her blouse and dropped sprinkles of water down there; then we all went to the door to watch, just as she got out ice cubes and put them in her pockets, us all howling out laughing, and her just kind of staring blank at us, you saying 'sweat, sweat,' until finally she wandered off into the utility room, and we found her in there with her blouse off, getting into the freezer. She had on a pink bra."

"That's when your parents came home."

"Yep. She was standing in the freezer when they walked in the door, back early from Thorndike." We sit quiet for a moment; he plugs the lamp into another cell, blinding me for a moment, the picture of Lawanda in the freezer bright in my memory, incarnate in the glare—her standing in the swirling zero air as stiffly as a zombie, apparently not intending to lie down in the chest but merely to stand there until she cooled off, or froze into an erotic statuette, a monument to my powers as a hypnotist, but looking strangely unfreezable in her pink bra, strangely flesh and blood, as my eyes fell upon a frilly patch of yellow organdy cut in the shape of a flower affixed between the cups of the bra, a decoration that was annoying to my Yucca-Flattened brains, somehow draining my sense of triumph with an abruptness that left me woozy—woozy and stupid, open mouthed, as Mr. and Mrs. Irwin walked in the door.

Mr. Irwin almost dropped his coke. Mrs. Irwin said, "Why *Lawanda Griggs*! You'll catch your death!"

"When they dragged her out, you acted like you were taking notes—remember that?"

"Don't tell me. I remember." I grabbed a pencil and pretended to be recording valuable scientific data, as if to thereby ennoble the experiment, to portray myself as a budding young psychiatrist, meanwhile trying to conjure some fast way to release her from the post-hypnotic suggestions without saying the termination signal in front of the Irwins, while Mr. Irwin paced around trying not to look at the sweating, groggy, partially undraped Lawanda, muttering to himself, "I've seen some things . . . I *have seen* some things, . . ." and Mary finally helped her on with the blouse. Mrs. Irwin left for a blanket, and I blurted the signal: "Presto piss water, pickles are poison," which Mr. Irwin unfortunately heard, stared in amazement as Lawanda came back to life, abandoned his coke to whoever took it, and walked away in deep abstraction, like a man suddenly deprived of his reality principle.

Johnny and I sit quietly for a moment, glum. He then knocks the snakes off the gig, the shit pond swallowing them with a faint lap.

"Where is Lawanda now?"

"Secretary in Little Rock; got a kid I think."

I reach into the water with both arms and release the motor from the cable. My face close, I detect now the smell of the pond, something like the cherry-colored floor-sweeping compound used in my grade school—ancient memory. The motor is free, and we are soon trolling along the edge, spotting for frogs.

As we approach, he takes shape, from the distant orange glow of a single eye to a fully embodied frog, squatting on the bank a foot from the water, larger than the two Johnny caught put together. He is flagrantly green in the light, an outrageously froglike frog, somehow like a dream frog, and I am to catch him. Johnny maneuvers the boat, whispers, "Snatch tight with both hands and throw him quick into the basket." We glide toward the bank, and I lean out over the front, opening my hands to snatch. He is pinned in the light, stone still, but squatting on muscular legs. "He's a jumper: don't diddle." The motor off, close to the shore, I lunge, grab cold meat, moist—gone.

"He jumped!"

"What'd you expect him to do?"

"Squeaked! Made a squeak like a rat. Frog's not supposed to squeak."

"You knocked the air out of him."

"Air? He jumped over my head, didn't he? Clear over. That sucker had legs."

"Naw, I believe he just kind of slipped down into the water. He'd a been dinner for four, that's for sure."

"Just too big, John, don't you think? Old and tough."

"Could be."

We patrol the remaining side of the shit pond and spot no more frogs. The plan now is to try Uncle Dwain's irrigation ditch, just across the pasture. We haul the dripping boat out and trudge through a herd of restive cows, Johnny rattling the boat to spook them: "Oooga booga! Oooga!" We set the boat down and rest. He tells me about Uncle Dwain's new Santa Gertrudis bull, lurking somewhere in this pasture, bought from Winthrop Rockefeller for ten thousand dollars. "Do you want to look for him?"

"What for?"

"To see him. He's pure chestnut and built like a tank. Rockefeller hangs just about as much meat as you can on a bull. That sucker looks like a meat mountain with a little old bitty face peeking out. There—see what I mean?" He spots the bull twenty yards from us, as if called up at will for my inspection (Johnny with his grace, his trademark, always there when the world is falling into place, as if he belonged solidly to the machinery of it—beating the train by few enough seconds to get a rise out of Mary, falling in somersaults, if he fell at all, from trick skis). He approaches the bull, and I follow, anxious—I don't know why—to be near the light. The bull is standing sideways to us, along a fence, and he doesn't move. Very close, we stop. He is so muscular that he looks uncomfortable, like a weight lifter who can't brush his teeth.

"Look at that sucker."

"Hadn't we better keep a ways back?"

"As long as we keep this light on him, he won't move. Here, take it and I'll show you." He hands me the lamp and approaches the beast. "Keep it in his eye and come up a little." He moves closer, circles the bull, now within reaching distance of the horns, and stops directly in front. The only movement is the bull's breath-

82

ing. Johnny reaches out slowly, crouched, ready to jump, his hand approaching the horn. He touches it, holds for a few seconds—mute tableau in white light—then releases.

"Hello Mr. Rockefeller, how you this evening?" he breathes. Ominously, slowly, the bull lowers his head. Johnny steps away. He takes the lamp from me. "Looked like he was starting to frown at me. Let's get over this fence."

We carry the boat to the irrigation ditch, slip and slide down a jungly bank, and launch it in brown dead water about fifteen feet wide, thick on both sides with cottonwood and brush. Mr. Cain's motor starts easily, and Johnny maneuvers us through the close passage, flashing into tangles of green for the eyes of frogs, which are promised by the very depth and luxuriance of it, green so fecund that it must be hiding something, as we skirt logs and brush, trolling a careful serpentine path, yet brushing limbs and half-hidden sticks that yield and scrape and bob with distant thuds beneath our feet. The motor cut, a glowing dot flickers, disappears, floating watery orange not quite embodied, like an imagined microbe swimming into my eye, and we glide through button willows, my face blinded, then a soft patch of mossy bank lit white with a frog that my hands leap, clutching, and throw into the metal net Johnny already holds out, and I wipe from my face the good itch of blood from a sticker's bite, pushing us out of the trees, ready for the next one. The slight buzz of dope worn off, clarity of deepening cooling night takes shape around my body, and I am eager now for what Johnny's light will illumine in the clustered gloom of the submerged waterway, almost anxious for it to penetrate farther ahead, where cattail and horseweed choke up the passage and cypress squat near the bank, frothy shadows of leaves filtering out the night sky. The caged frogs jingle, clangle across the floor, bashing against the metal on legs that spring repeatedly, rhythmically, themselves seeking freedom. I lay the gig on top of the cage.

"You'll need it for this one."

"How do I?"

"Just stab him."

"Any old place?"

The motor cut, we nose into a tree, and I spot him, medium sized, and shove the gig through branches, lunging, missing again. He sits placidly behind a branch, transfixed even in half-light, as if dreamily reconciled to the barbs. I try from the other side of the branch. . . .

"Here." Johnny, on the middle seat, takes the gig, pulls the boat around, and in one easy motion jabs the frog, which leaps in four directions like a cheerleader, then shrinks around the steel. I tear him loose, in the exaggerated light, blood oozing carmine from two ragged holes—one between its eyes—like blood in a cheap Technicolor movie. In the cage, they all jump when he is plopped into their midst, and he jumps even more wildly, not knowing he is dead, which gives me the creeps. "I bet if you chopped one of those things in two, they'd grow a new end—either end."

"No, they won't, but I'll tell you one thing they will do. Unless you take out the leg nerve when you're cleaning them, they'll hop out of the frying pan and jump around the floor. It's the grossest thing I ever saw. I once had to chase one down—hopped nearly into the living room, dripping hot grease. That sucker had a crust on him, and he up and decided he didn't want to be cooked after all and would take a last crack at getting back to the pond."

"And you gobbled him down, and he started hopping around in your stomach, hopped down your bowels and jumped out your ass hole."

"I ain't shitting you, Alder. I threw him to the dogs."

"And they hopped off into the moonlight, howling and hopping."

"Don't give me a hard time now. My head still feels a little expanded."

Farther on, the ditch shallower, Johnny steps out and pushes the boat, as I spot straight ahead, the banks close. A snake cruises toward us. "Gig that sucker."

I don't; it's a water snake, not a moccasin, and not about to hurt anybody, but Johnny splashes alongside, kicking up water to turn

it back, and wades after it, stabbing the water, disappearing through
a cypress. Silence.

"I can't see. Get the light up here."

"I'm stuck. Lost my motor."

"Well paddle."

I try but really am stuck. He emerges from the branches and
stands in the light, ankle deep in water. "I think we're done for
here. This ditch is gave out."

"Stops dead?"

"Not dead, but it's too narrow to get a boat up."

"And that water snake got away?" I hold the dimming light
on him, as he stands now in profile staring into green. A connection
inside me is deeply askew, vague yet insistent, like eyes on the back
of my head. I get out of the boat and walk toward him with the
battery and lamp.

"What you doing?"

"Looking around."

I shine the bank, his face—then push through branches and
emerge in the open.

"What you doing?"

The ditch ahead is puddled mud with a narrow stream in the
middle. "Chasing snakes," I hear myself saying.

He is silent.

"Come on."

"I didn't think you liked to kill snakes."

"I want to kill a moccasin. You got the gig—now come on."

He comes through the curtain of cypress. "Ain't much water
up there."

"Doesn't need to be; I just want to find me a *big old fat snake*.
Come on." We start up the creek bed, globbing through mud that
sucks like a plumber's helper and adheres to our shoes in ponderous
chunks. I lead the way, hurtle into a stand of button willow and
am bitten, nicked in five places by thorns, the battery wires tangling,
as Johnny thrashes along behind with no light, and I imagine tree
snakes slipping from limbs, angling face level out of the dark. After

a bend the ditch narrows, and we are forced to walk in a shallow channel of water, pushing through cobwebs, bushes, sticks. I turn and walk backward through some cattail, giving Johnny light for a moment, and suddenly find myself stepped off into deeper water. It is a pool. A glance of the weakening light reveals that it is wide— say a hundred feet—and without brush except for a dead tree hulking near the opposite bank. Haze clings to the surface—more smoke than haze—and I shine my feet: the water, knee deep, is white. Pure white. I step out as Johnny emerges.

"This water is white."

"Goddamn, I got a horseweed up my nose. . . ."

"Look at that. What caused it to be that way?"

He blasts out his nostril and picks it. "I don't know."

I am shining the water nearby and thinking it looks like skim milk when suddenly a bubble erupts—a single immense bubble in the very place that I am spotting—as if I had known that there would be a bubble and exactly where.

"Alder, I just had a hallucination."

"Did we circle back to another shit pond? It looks like chemicals."

"I wish I had my .30–.30." He takes the lamp from me and spots the pond, moving slowly around the edge—then stops, crouches . . . moves backwards. I step up behind him. He whispers, "You don't need to send me any of that marahoochie after all."

"What?"

"Look right down on the mud where I'm shining. See it? Tell me you do, now."

I do see it—only a few paces away: a white frog, pure white, just like the pond, squatting on the bank.

Johnny switches the light off, then on. "A spook if I ever saw one. Don't ever let me smoke that stuff again."

"It's an albino. Must be. An albino frog."

Bladoop the pond burps again. The frog does not move.

"Eyes ain't red."

"They seem blue."

"I can't tell." We peer at it: medium sized, sitting at a slight angle from the water, hunkered down as if sleeping, not even thinking of jumping. "Let's get that sucker."

"No."

He turns. "Huh?"

"You can't kill an albino."

"What?"

"You can't do it." I am touching his shoulder.

Bladoop.

"If I didn't carry that thing home to show, Mary and everybody else would have me by the balls. I ain't ever heard of a white frog. Come on."

I jerk the lamp wire loose. Darkness. But in a moment the frog reappears, glowing blue white, unmoving.

"What'd you do that for?" He sets down the extinguished lamp and approaches the frog. I run past him and try to scare it away. But it must be the stupidest white frog in the world, because it doesn't hop. Johnny moves around me, hands outstretched. I tackle him belly level, *splug,* land left shoulder in soft deep mud, jackknife and cover him, sit on him, and hold his arms down, no resistance, his head ear deep, ensconced neatly in the muck. "*Aalder?* . . . That's like little old *kids.* You put me down in the *mud.*" His belly heaves, and I roll toward the frog, him jumping me now, and I struggle, arm thrown to scare it away, but he grabs my hand, mud squishing between our fingers, and peers down through darkness at me. Our faces close. "That frog is deader 'n a doornail. I don't know what you're getting us all muddy for."

"*Dead?*"

"Ain't just dead, he's dead and bleached. I just figured it out." He gets up and kicks the frog. It flips over but does not alter its squat. It is between us, and Johnny spots it with the lamp after reconnecting the dying battery.

I finally stand up, fingering a clot of mud in my ear. "It looks like a piece of marble."

He looks up, a bent stick dangling from a squab of mud in his hair, and his forehead muddy, expression blank, looking not at me but through me into his own mind, his voice from somewhere else, "I figure this is where Uncle Dwain dumped some extra bean poison, and that burp is a lump of it down there melting. This frog got bleached and crawled out in time to die."

"What kind of bean poison?"

"I don't know anything about beans, not even the first thing."

"Maybe it's another shit pond—if we came in a circle. . . ."

"Maybe." He wipes a glob from his elbow and thwaps it onto the mud.

Bladoop.

"Come on now, goddamn it Johnny, I know we're too old to wallow in the mud. . . ."

"Ain't too old to do anything. You been trying to teach me that all night—just like Mary giving me that shit all the time. I tell her just like I'll tell you, there isn't any such a thing as 'too old' for me, because the minute I start thinking like that I don't do *nothing* but get messed up. I'll corn hole the cow just like I did when I was thirteen if I by God want to, and the day I'm too old to kill a snake is the day I'll give up. I don't mind tussling either; I practically taught you how to do that if you'll remember. First time you came down here you were the weirdest sucker I ever saw. I had to convince you to get it on with Lawanda Griggs that first time. You remember that? Like I say, I don't mind tussling, but *goddamn* Alder, you ought not to throw me down in the mud when I'm not looking." He kicks the frog into the pond. "And another thing: you're the one hadn't got any older—got a mop on your head but that's about the only difference. Now you want to gig some frogs or not?"

"That's what we came for."

"There's another ditch in that direction, close, and I know where it goes. Let's see if we can't get the boat to it."

We trudge back, lightless, then struggle the boat through a tangle of bushes, him at the front and me at the back. The other ditch is wider and deeper, but in an hour we gig only one frog. Hauling the boat out the last time is easier, up a gentle slope covered in weeds. The sky is clouded over completely, rain long imminent now forming in the smell and feel of the air. I have no sense of direction after travelling the indefinitely meandering ditches, but Johnny seems to know where we are. He disappears, and in a moment the unmistakable Green Goose clatters to life—so close that I jump—and headlights ignite a stand of green.

6

THE BULLET

I was six years old the day I got to ride the stock elevator with Grandfather Slate. He talked to me that day for the first and only time, although he lived another fourteen years, in his right mind until the very hour that he walked out of Slate Wholesale Hardware and got into his '48 Plymouth, put it in second (he never used first), and drove from the parking lot straight across the street, over the curb and up the lawn of the old courthouse, cracked the axle of a Yankee cannon, and ran head-on into the brick wall of the building, knocking a handful of shingles loose from the ceiling and shattering a courtroom window that the Park Service proudly claimed had been there since 1876, when Judge Isaac C. Parker sentenced his first hanging. In the letter I received at college, Mother said the family was proud that he had gone to work on his last day. She said that he had apparently suffered a stroke after starting the car. I doubted that—one reason why I had to go off by myself to digest the letter.

My father was with me at Slate Hardware that afternoon in 1952—it was a Saturday—going over some orders and having a conference with Austen Slate, Jr., about borrowing money for our new house. I wandered into the dusty high-ceilinged office that Grandfather Slate had occupied as president for thirty-fiive years and that doubled as an auxiliary sporting-goods stockroom. I wanted to see the Winchester bullet display, not Grandfather, who seemed to be from another planet, a dried-up old lizard man with incongruous wet red eyes that floated behind his face, and utterly slow movements, as if his bones were summer weeds threatening to snap. He was so careful with each movement that he made me impatient, made me want to dance around him, and say, "Grandfather, get a move on!" I knew that was impossible, so I usually tried to avoid him. That day he was asleep on the black leather couch that stood between gloomy shelves of fishing lures and spinning reels, lying with his hands clasped on his stomach. He looked like he would never move. On the wall above a rolltop desk was the display, with thirty-six bullets and shells on it, including an eight-gauge shotgun shell, cutaways showing powder and wadding and a cowboy killing a huge, slavering grizzly bear in the background. It was irresistible, especially the eight-gauge shell, which my brother had told me could knock down a brick wall (I did not know then that not even my grandfather's Plymouth could knock down a brick wall), and I stood on the desk chair to see it more closely, touching it when his raspy whisper scared me nearly into midair, "Have to prop an eight-gauge or it will bust you."

I must have crouched to jump, because children were not supposed to climb on furniture, but he did not order me off. Instead he sat on the edge of the couch, put his pipe into his mouth, and told me about the time he dislocated his shoulder at a turkey shoot with an eight-gauge. He spoke the tale quietly into the gloom, not noticing me standing fixed on the chair, until he'd finished, when he took the pipe out of his mouth and looked at me with a smile that cracked his old lizard face and showed two yellow teeth. "And it hurt when John Harper set it, too. Served a young buck right. I had to eat that turkey in a sling."

And then we were on the elevator in the stockroom, a huge platform of splintery greasy planks, open on all sides so that you could see into the labyrinths of general hardware—stoves, rakes, fans, hinges, lawn mowers, guns, fishing boats, kegs of nails, bullets, toasters, toilets, hammers, shears, chicken wire, lightning rods—as we glided upward toward a dark hole swallowing the cable in the topmost ceiling. There was a black man up there who rolled the oily steel rope onto a wooden spindle. He waited for Grandfather's signal. I feared that we would not stop and the hole would swallow us. Then we would have to walk down a steep crooked staircase with no banister and crawl through holes and small doors to get out. Or if he did not pull the rope that he held with his funny old cricket hand, we would squash against the ceiling and then fall six floors. I would have to jump just as we hit bottom to keep from getting killed. I wanted to help him pull the rope in time, but if I moved my weight, the platform might lose its balance, for there were no walls around it. I held as still as I could, my heart pumping, ready to save my life. The elevator stopped a good two feet above the top floor; he pulled the other rope and we descended below the rafters. My stomach came up my throat when he cursed, and I was just about to vault to safety when he jiggled the ropes and inched us level with the floor.

Walking past shelves and shelves of dry-smelling rope, I avoided cracks between the planks wide enough to see through to the floor below us. Grandfather stopped beside a spindle of white cord that stood as tall as me and twice as round. He cursed it, then took out a match and lit the end of the cord and held it while it sizzled. I backed away, again uneasy, and asked him if that was dynamite.

"Hell no, it's a piece of nylon rope. Think I'd blow up my own store? You should always close off nylon after you cut it or it will frazzle out. Damn kids don't respect the stock—no use telling me they do. Come over here and I'll tell you about dynamite." At the window we were so high—five stories high—that we could see the Arkansas River curve and curve like a snake. I already knew that Oklahoma was on the other side. "That river coming into the Arkansas is the Poteau. You ever hear of that?"

"No."

"Well it is. We got our drinking water out of it during the war . . . I don't know which one . . . I guess the first one. Brown as a cow pond. They called it Poteau Punch. Drink too much of it and you'd get constipated. Look over there—pay attention—about a half mile up the Poteau was where we kept our dynamite. You see over there?"

"I don't see anything."

"Ain't anything to see. It blew up in 1897. I was twenty years old the day it blew up, and we ain't had a powder house since."

I looked and looked out the window, not knowing what to say.

"There were three people over there fishing, and they couldn't find any part of them. Blew them to smithereens as far as anybody could tell. I was riding the ferry back across the river after a week of selling pots and pans to the Indians. Damn Indians were the best customers we ever had. They would buy pots and pans, and then a week later they'd buy some more. One winter I found out they were using them for sleds, sitting in them, and holding the handle and sliding down the hills. I caught a grown Cherokee, the son of a customer of mine, ran a little store in Oneeta, name of Frank Sad Horse. I won't forget the old coot, must have been two hundred years old. Twice as old as I am. . . ."

Grandfather was no longer talking to me. He was looking out the window toward Oklahoma. I asked him what he had caught Frank Sad Horse's son at.

"Sliding down a hill—I already told you—in a sixteen-inch frying pan. I peed in my pants I laughed so hard. Young Frank didn't like it either. I don't know why, I guess I got his pride up. I was a buck then myself. Old Frank used to have a slave, a nigger the name of Wick that stayed with him after the War Between the States. He and old Frank played checkers, far as I could tell, day and night. The slowest checkers players I ever saw, they could sit there and think about the next move long enough for me to take stock, write up a two-page order and maybe sell him the newest stove out of Cleveland. I never did see them move once. Wick was on the ball though. I'd trade him for any three white men we got down there right now. He talked Cherokee, Creek, Choctaw, and I wouldn't doubt Apache. I would have carried him along with me to sell hardware if he'd left Frank." He stared out the window, his pipe in his mouth, under the bowl a drop of saliva forming that sparkled yellow in dust-filtered sunlight. I looked at the cannon on the old courthouse lawn, wondering if we could get one like it to put in the front yard of our new house. A cannon would be just right. I would polish it everyday and roll it up to the house when it rained.

He was looking down at me. "What was I talking about, Austen?"

I did not know how to say what he was talking about.

"Pay attention now boy. You were asking me about the fishermen that got blown up over on the Poteau. One of them was a no-good Indian and two of them were no-good white men, so it didn't matter too much. The kind that would be catfishing on a workday. My father put on a good funeral for them, anyway—fact of the matter, he put on a separate funeral for all three of them. Mock funeral I guess it was, since they couldn't find any part of them. He did it right, too. Had every damn employee of Slate Hardware down to the messenger boy go to their funerals to pay respects. Had them all on the same day. At one of them there wasn't anything but Slate Hardware there. Relatives were probably glad we blew him up. I was on the ferry coming back from a selling trip when it happened. A ball of fire come up in the sky and Witty Radder that ran the ferry fell onto his knees—he was some kind of Mennonite, I think—and started mumbling and praying like it was a fast-talking contest. I never heard a word he said, but I reckon God would have taken mercy on him for all the effort he was putting out. The sound didn't come until the fire had grabbed itself together in a ball and turned scarlet. It hit you in the face like a baseball, cracked or blew out most of the windows on the south side of Garrison. That afternoon my father had me carry tape around to all the different places where there was still some window left. Nobody cussed me but a Chinese barber, and I couldn't understand him. Everybody was standing in the street, talking, and comparing windows. That was the friendliest I saw this town. My name was Austen Slate and they knew Slate powder house had just blew out all their windows, but they didn't cuss me. I guess that was the day this town got civilized."

I asked him what "civilized" meant.

He took the pipe from his mouth and tapped out the burned

load in his palm. "That's when people get along." He handed me the palmful of ash and burned tobacco. "Hold that for me until I find a wastebasket. Can't put ashes on the floor."

He walked over to a shelf and pulled out a brown carton with Daisy Red Rider printed on the end of it. I knew what that was, and my heart started beating fast. "Did you ever shoot a BB gun?" he asked.

"No sir, but I can. I can do it. My brother did it. I can shoot a cannon, too, if I want to."

"We'll see about that." He opened the box and took out the gun. The barrel was black and oily and the stock wooden, engraved with Red Rider on a horse. He opened one of the two packages of BBs in the box and carefully poured them click clicking into the magazine. "All right, what will be our target?"

I put the handful of ashes and burned tobacco into my pocket and looked around. "You mean we'll shoot in here?"

"No, has to be outside; might break something in here. Only place you can shoot inside the store is the basement. Look out there and see if you can see something that won't be broke." He handed me the gun and unlocked the window, cobwebs and dust puffing up as he opened it. We decided to shoot at the metal plaque beside the Yankee cannon. I did not know it then, but the sign explained that the cannon was a remnant of the capture of Fort Smith in 1863 by Brig. Gen. James C. Blount, who remained until the end of the war, "undertaking punitive actions against the Indians who sympathized with the Confederacy." And I did not know that in fourteen years Grandfather would get into his car and black out and then smash the wheel off this very cannon, as though in some mystic completion of our target practice. We took turns. He let me cock the gun for myself and did not tell me how to aim, and so I missed and was jealous of the distant *ping* that a few of his shots brought. Then he loaded his pipe and sat on the edge of a shelf, allowing me to shoot alone. I kept missing, cocking and shooting, cocking and shooting, getting more impatient, until he told me to take it easy, I was liable to break a window. I was mad and delighted and voracious to hit the plaque. That *ping* would have been the highest accomplishment in the world. Higher than being able to roll my stomach like my brother, higher even than having a rubbery neck like an Egyptian dancer, an ability that I had daydreamed about forever and asked for repeatedly, with no luck, in the private prayer that I added onto the Lord's Prayer each night at bedtime. Yes, I would have foolishly traded one *ping* for that marvelous ability, would have done it in an instant, but I could not at that moment tell God, because praying in the daytime was out of the question. It occurred to me—I will admit it—but I did not actually go through with it. God had a lot to do in the daytime and would not take lightly to being interrupted.

So I just kept peppering the front lawn of the old courthouse, while Grandfather sat there huffing little clouds of Prince Albert, more smell than smoke, staring off into some ancient memory—or perhaps into nothing at all. Once he asked me if there was anybody out there; I told him no and he said good, he didn't want anybody shooting back. The old courthouse was not yet a national monument then, so there was no reason for people to be wandering around this oldest and deadest part of town. In a few years they would come in droves to see the courthouse where Isaac Parker sentenced more than a hundred-fifty men to be hanged, and to take pictures of the reconstructed gallows, a whitewashed platform built to take sixteen at a time, and to sniff the dank air of the underground jail, which two hundred U.S. marshals at once tried to keep full, from the time Grandfather was born in 1877 through the late nineties, combing seventy-four thousand square miles of Indian Territory for whiskey peddlars, burglars, train robbers, and murderers—themselves just as crooked as their prey, because six cents a mile and two dollars for an encounter that "endangered life and limb" was not enough to live on. I did not know any of it then, but Grandfather planted a seed of interest in me that day. At some moment in my fever of trying to hit the plaque, perhaps when I was debating whether to ask God for help, he mentioned Belle Starr. He said that he had seen her once at a Fort Smith fair, where they had hired her for local color. He said that she rode sidesaddle and was ugly as a mud fence. And he spoke of Pearl Younger, Belle's bastard daughter by Cole Younger, and said that nobody knew it—again musing to himself between puffs—but Pearl's Hotel was still standing down where First Street used to be.

"Nobody knows it," he repeated, "or they've all forgot it, but that old hotel is still standing just as high as it was in 1890 when my mother told me that if I got anywhere near First Street at night, I would forfeit my soul to the devil and burn in hell for eternity."

I asked Grandfather what that meant. I had not yet learned that side of theology. Although I knew—or instinctively felt—that God could get angry and punish evildoers, I did not yet know that there was a separate and individual power to take care of such matters. I felt that God could take care of it all. Grandfather did not answer, and I asked him again. He still did not answer. His pipe had gone out, and he was sitting very still on the shelf, not looking at me. He was not looking at anything. From the small of my back ice water rose to my brain. I turned away from him and cocked the BB gun.

*   *   *

It was sometime in high school that I first saw Pearl's Hotel. I had not thought of it or even remembered Grandfather's mention of it for many years—but seeing it, I knew without question that it was Pearl Younger's hotel. Standing across the switch tracks against the Arkansas River floodwall, with no other buildings nearby, it was square, two storied, with a modest Greek cornice above the front door, and, strangely, a brand new coat of white paint. I later discovered that the Park Service—or rather one passionately idealistic ranger by the name of Red Puller—was trying to renovate the building and open it as a part of the monument. He was naturally having some trouble convincing the U.S. government to buy an old whorehouse and display it as a national monument, but he had meanwhile taken it upon himself to finance the painting and was trying to round up a Citizen's Committee to Save Pearl Younger's Hotel, a zealous but misguided project for which he earned the title "that idiot Park Ranger" among the moderate citizens and the desire—among the more upright ones—to hang him on his own newly reconstructed gallows. He had red hair and buckteeth and worked day and night to reconstruct Fort Smith's history, digging in old records, discovering foundations that had been buried and forgotten for a hundred years, advertising in the newspaper for "elderly Fort Smithians who recall facts about the city from before 1900," begging old law firms for probate records, flying to Washington on his vacation to read Zachary Taylor's memoirs of Fort Smith, even writing letters to a library in Spain for details on La Salle's journey up the Arkansas River. Red Puller was not a Park Ranger, he was a scholar, and it was from him that I learned what Grandfather did not teach me on the day that we shot the BB gun. I would never have mentioned that incident to Red, as he would doubtless have delivered me a stern and endless lecture on Defiling Public Monuments, even though it had happened ten years before—wiping his face with a dark green handkerchief, as he always did, and smiling toothily at odd moments in his monologue. He talked only in monologue, and although I never witnessed one of his interviews with an "elderly citizen who remembers facts," I can safely imagine that he told them more than they told him. He spoke a running barrage of facts, endless details from old plans and records and speeches and newspapers, raw chunks of old Fort Smith gobbled whole, undigested, regurgitated in nineteenth-century phrases, as though he were a living witness to the last century, always just arrived from a journey back in his time-warped mind. He did not seem to enjoy it. There was always heartburn in his face—perhaps not real heartburn, but a kind of psychic heartburn that caused fleeting but regular looks of discomfort—so that his face was always punctuated with smiles, heartburn, and wipes of the green handkerchief, all at the wrong time and with no sense of climax, as he kept up his endless narrative about the Fort Smith that Grandfather was raised in but did not tell me about, as he sat there, and will always sit in my memory, dead still on a shelf in the musty silent fifth floor of Slate Hardware.

Red loved to talk about the seventy-nine men who actually hanged on the gallows. That one lit him up like a pinball machine. He remembered them in chronological order: Daniel Evans, William Whittington, James Moore, Smoker Mankiller, Sam Fooy, and Edmund Campbell, the first six to hang, 3 September 1875; Orpheus McGee, who lured Robert Alexander from his cabin by gobbling like a wild turkey and shot him through the face with a Winchester rifle on 20 April 1874; Dr. Henri Stewart, who had studied medicine at Harvard and become a noted physician, but later ignominiously abandoned his family of five and ran away to Indian Territory to become a train robber, killing J.B. Jones in an attempted holdup at Caddo, Choctaw Nation, in 1879; Edward Fulsom, a man of such slight build that his pulse beat for one hour and three minutes after the trap had sprung; Famous Smith, who murdered the innocent industrious white farmer Nathaniel Hyatt, mutilating his physiognomy beyond recognition, a deed that surely foreordained his doom in the fiery regions; Tualisto, a Creek Indian who robbed and killed a travelling salesman for money to go to a green-corn dance, suffering his just retribution at the tribal whipping post and at the gallows in Fort Smith, where, just before he left this world, he bragged that each of the four red buttons on his hat represented a man he had killed; a part-Cherokee named Kit Ross, who responded out loud to Judge Parker's fatal sentence, "Well, they done it to me"; Gus Bogles, who in the summer of 1887 killed a man named J.D. Morgan by buckling a strap around his neck and belaboring him with a pistol; a fractious and discourteous prisoner, Bogles tried twice to seize a guard's pistol and once to smuggle himself out of jail in a barrel that had contained sawdust for spittoons, and on his last night he screamed and whooped for no other reason than to annoy his fellow prisoners; Bood Crumpton, who at the youthful age of nineteen shot a friend in the back and dumped his body in a pit near the Pawnee Indian Agency, and whose message from the gallows was doubtless a potent lesson to many a lawless inebriate: "To all you who are present, especially the young men—the next time you are about to take a drink of whiskey, look closely into the bottom of the glass and see if you cannot observe in there a hangman's noose. There is where I first saw the one which now breaks my neck"; John Thornton, who committed one of the most egregious crimes ever recorded at Judge Parker's court, repeatedly and mercilessly violating his own daughter, a thin and trembling blonde who at a tender age married to escape her father's revolting abuse and was killed by him in the absence of her husband, Thornton emptying a pistol into her body, such a fat and flabby man that when he dropped at the end of a rope blood spurted as the flesh of his neck ripped apart, causing the crowd to shudder with horror, and three elderly ladies, who had come together from Towsend Street, to faint in unison at the abhorrent sight; Lewis Holder, who robbed and murdered his business associate, dumping his shotgun-riddled body in a gorge in the Choctaw Nation, 28 December 1891, such a cowardly man that upon Judge Parker's pronouncement that he "be hanged by the neck until dead," his face turned an ashen color, a violent tremor shook his body, and he let out a scream that was heard in the street outside, and even, one report has it, inside the Slate Hardware Company building some fifty yards away (I interrupted here, asking Red who heard the scream; was it my grandfather? He did not know, as only one of the four newspaper articles on the event carried the scream all the way to Slate Hardware, and they were vague about it), then he fell to the floor and remained so unresponsive that many thought he had cheated the gallows, but he had not, and awaiting the final day, he begged the guards passing his cell not to hang him, finally threatening that he would return as a spirit and haunt them—even this failing to stay the hand of justice, although later reports had it that indeed some nights unearthly sounds did float from the inky darkness that enveloped the gallows, startling jailers and prisoners alike. And there were the big ones, the gangs— the Starrs, the Daltons, the Rogers, the Cooks, the Bucks. . . .

I listened closely to Red when he spoke of the Bucks, the most depraved outlaws in Indian Territory, a band of five led by Rufus Buck, a full-blooded Euchee Indian, including Sam Sampson and Maoma July, Creek desperados, and Lewis and Lucky Davis, Creek freedmen—a mixture of Negro and Creek, doubtless the most vicious of all types of mixed-blood outlaws—who in thirteen days rampaged across the Creek Nation, robbing stores, stealing cattle, shooting a young Negro boy, killing a Negro deputy marshal, and committing multiple rapes upon an Indian and a white woman, finally being apprehended after a shoot-out with a posse of Creek Lighthorsemen and brought to Fort Smith, where the rape of the white woman Rosetta Hassan somehow took precedence over the murder of the Negro deputy, and the wounding of the Negro boy, and rape of the Indian woman, as the indictment that was drawn up stated that Rufus Buck and Lewis Davis and Lucky Davis and Sam Sampson and Maoma July, on the fifth day of August, A.D., 1895, at the Creek Nation, in the Indian country, within the Western District of Arkansas aforesaid, in and upon Rosetta Hassan, a white woman, and not an Indian, feloniously, did ravish and carnally know, contrary to the form of the statute in such case made and provided, and the peace and dignity of the United States of America—the thereby indicted Bucks brought to trial, where the white woman who had been raped—a beautiful and modest woman of thirty years, well proportioned and with a look that betokened a kindly disposition, dressed in nothing that could have been considered gaudy, with skin, it was said, so white that it was almost ghostly—this woman forced upon the witness stand to describe the outrage committed upon her by Lucky Davis, the colored brute who had held the muzzle of a Winchester to her forehead and forced her to lie down, testimony which caused the entire courtroom, packed with irate citizens, including representatives from several civic groups, to shed noble and sympathetic tears, of which no one of them was ashamed, not the rough-and-ready deputies, nor even Judge Parker, who, notwithstanding his inurement to brutal crimes through long years on the bench, removed his spectacles and was said to have had a suspicious moisture glistening upon his eyelashes, and the attorney appointed for the defence William M. Cravens, knowing the feeling among the citizenry, stood and said, in what was probably the shortest plea for defence ever recorded, May it please the court and you, gentlemen of the jury, you have heard the evidence. I have nohting to say. And Judge Parker, after the verdict, said to the criminals, The offence of which you have been convicted is one which shocks all men who are not brutal. It is known to the law as a crime offensive to decency, and as a brutal attack upon the honor and chastity of the weaker sex. It is a violation of the quick sense of honor and the pride of virtue which nature, to render the sex amiable, has implanted in the female heart. And on 1 July 1896, the five were led from the underground cell below the courthouse, all perfectly calm, clad in black suits, Maoma July and Lucky Davis wearing large boutonnieres upon the left lapel of their coats, ascending the steps of the gallows and sitting upon the bench while the death warrant was read, after which they stood and Lucky Davis shouted good-bye, Martha to his sister, who was present, and Rufus Buck's father, a big, heavy old man, got into the jail enclosure and attempted to come up the steps to the platform where his son stood, but, stupidly drunk, he was escorted below. And the condemned stepped forward, none of them showing signs of fear except Lucky Davis, whose face twitched in nervousness as the black cap was placed over his head, and at 1:28 P.M. the trap dropped with its hideous chug and Lewis Davis died in three minutes, his neck broken, as were the necks of Sam Sampson and Maoma July, Rufus Buck, and Lucky Davis being strangled to death, Davis's body drawing up several times before it straightened out. And in Rufus Buck's cell, after the execution, was found a photograph of the criminal's mother with a bizarre farewell poem that the condemned had written on the back—a copy of which being the only memento that Red Puller ever gave me, not needing to give me anything else, since he repeated his histories often enough that I could never forget them, not if I tried, for they run in my mind some nights like a muddy river, like the Arkansas River, and there is no stopping them. I forget about Rufus Buck's poem. But then I happen upon it in the back of a drawer and re-read it. At the top right-hand corner of the page is the sketch of a braceleted arm with the forefinger pointing at the title: "MY, dream—1896"; at the bottom of the page is the sketch of a tomb made of natural rock with ivy growing around the base of the cross; above the ivy, across the page is written "virtue and resurrection"; on the cross:

```
            H
            O
            L
            Y
FATHER   SON
            G
            H
            O
            S
            T
```

The poem, above the tomb, reads:

> i, dremp't, i, WAS, in, HeAVen,
> Among, THe, AngelS, Fair;
> i'd, neAr, seen, none, So, HAndSome,
> THAT, TWine, in, goLden, HAir;
>   THey, Looked, So, neat, And SAng, So, Sweet,
> And, Play,d, THe, THe, goLden, HArp,
> i, wAs, ABout, To, pick, An, Angel, ouT,
> And, TAke, Her, To, mY, HeArT;
>   BuT, THe, momenT, i, BegAn, To PleA,
> i, THougHT, oF, You, mY, LOVE,
> THere, WAS, none, i'd, Seen, So, BeauTiFuLL,
> On, eArTH, or, HeAVen, ABove.
> gooD, By, My, Dear, WIFe, anD, MoTher.

I Day. of. JUly   all. so. My. sisTers
Tu, THe, Yeore   RUFUS, BUCK
off   Youse, Truley
1896

*   *   *

There was another souvenir—given to me by Grandfather on the day we shot the BB gun. It was a .44 caliber bullet taken from the bandolier Belle Starr was wearing the day she was killed. Apparently, it had been given to Grandfather by his father, who had received it from George Maledon, Judge Parker's hangman. Maledon probably got it from one of the deputies investigating Belle Starr's murder. I heard much later, from a second cousin, that Grandfather's father and Maledon were buddies. The immediate family was ashamed that Great-Grandfather was the friend of a hangman, and it was seldom mentioned. When I showed the bullet to Red Puller, he denied that it could have been Belle Starr's. He said that she did not have a .44 caliber gun—that she had never had one as far as he knew. I think the truth of the matter was that Red coveted that bullet and was altering the facts a little so I'd think it was worthless and just leave it with him.

But I couldn't do that. Belle Starr's bullet was always special—and a little weird.

Because Grandfather was bribing me when he gave me that bullet. We had to go back downstairs, but first Grandfather had to wake up. He had spells; that's what they called them later. At first, he seemed to be asleep with his eyes open. I still had not hit the sign, but I figured we should be going back down the elevator—if it went down. I only knew for sure that it went up. I knew a real elevator went down, too, but this was not a real one. It was too wide and had no walls, and you could almost feel a wind blowing when it rode you through the darkness. Grandfather had a spell before we went down. He sat there without moving, and I did not know what to say, because it was impolite to tell grown-ups when to leave. There was a drip of saliva under the bowl of his pipe, and he was staring into space without expression. The sun was going down. It occurred to me that he might be deciding whether to give me the BB gun, so I put it back into the box and stared at it lovingly. Grandfather stood up and my heart jumped. I figured he was going to give it to me. But he walked past me and down the aisle without saying anything, and I followed, disappointed to have left the BB gun. He stopped near a wall where there were garden plows hanging on nails. Then he took off his coat and hung it on a plow. That seemed strange. Then he took off his shirt. His back was to me, and I could not tell what he was doing until he had taken it off. In the gloom his back was stark white. He turned around and walked toward me, and I did not move. He sat on a shelf and began taking his shoes off. There was something funny about the way he was moving. He moved like there was nothing holding him back, as if he were suddenly not an old man. Or maybe not any man, maybe something more like the dream men who wandered in the different air of my sleep. His socks were thin bands of faded scarlet, which he took off and stuffed carefully into his shoes. His splayed skinny toes seemed to work and spread at odd angles when he stood up. Then he took off his pants, folding, and carefully placing them on a box of ax handles. He stood in orange dust light in underwear with faded candy canes running at angles on them. His lizard eyes were floating in another world. I tried to move behind the large spindle of rope, but I feared that he would awaken and be ashamed and I would be ashamed. I knew he was asleep, or gone somewhere, and I should not disturb him. I did not want him to take off his shorts, but he did. His little fluff of hair was red, and the idea came to me that they must be red when people were old.

He looked through me and said, "Nora, put on the comfort. It's cold tonight."

I did not move.

Then he went to the plows and unhooked something and put it on his legs—only there was nothing there—and he unhooked another nothing and put it on his top, rapidly buttoning imaginary buttons. And he lay down on the splintery pitted planks of the floor and said, "Good night, Nora." Nora was Grandmother, but she was dead and not there. She slept under the green lawn by the Arkansas River; that was where dead people went, and they stayed there—I was pretty sure of that. Maybe Grandfather was pretending that he was at the green lawn. But he did not pretend; no big people pretended. When his eyes shut and his face went to sleep, I could move. I went behind the spindle and hid, but the room was getting darker, and when I looked out at Grandfather, he seemed to be settling into the dust of the floor. I did not want him to disappear, because then he would be everywhere in the spreading darkness of the room. If he disappeared, I could not tell where he was. If he put his clothes back on, he would not disappear, and so I wished them back on him, but they did not go. Then I prayed, saying the Lord's Prayer very fast so I could get to the personal one at the end and ask God to put Grandfather's clothes back on. It was dark enough to pray now.

God did not put Grandfather's clothes back on.

The smell of rope, and of the dust of a hundred years, and the darkness that was spreading from corners and shelves all seemed to diminish at once, as my nose was filled with the charred wet briarwood redolence of Grandfather's pipe. It swarmed in my nose like something alive and diffused into my cheeks, and for a moment I was dizzy. I could not see the pipe. I wanted to see it and take it and put it under my nose and smell it again. I would give it to Grandfather and he would awaken. He always put his pipe in his mouth when he awakened. When he lit it, he came to life. I would help him. I went to his coat and found the pipe in a side pocket, then knelt beside him. I stuck my nose in the bowl of the pipe and smelled as hard as I could. His face was so asleep that it would be wrong to awaken him. I would get into trouble. But soon the room would be all dark, and the man who rolled the elevator up and down would go home for the night, and we would be stuck here. Grandfather's face was purple with sleep.

I said, "Grandfather, will you smoke your pipe?"

He did not move. So I put the pipe into his mouth, not touching his lips, but prying them apart with the stem and pushing it in. When it was upright in his mouth, I let go. It fell to the floor and lay in a crack between planks. I grabbed it and stuck it into his mouth again, wincing as it clinked against a tooth. I held it upright and said, "Grandfather, will you wake up and smoke your pipe?"

He did not do it.

I said, "God, will you wake Grandfather up and make him smoke his pipe." That was the first time I had ever talked to God out loud in my own words. God waited a few moments, as I continued to hold the pipe, then woke Grandfather up. His eyes switched open, and I could feel the grip of his mouth harden around the pipe. He propped himself up and took something out of the air and examined it. "Six-thirty," he said and stood up, the pipe still in his mouth, and put his clothes back on. When his coat was on, he stared at the wall of garden plows. His hand reached up as if to touch one of them, but it did not. He turned, his hand still held out. "What are you doing here . . . boy?"

I could not answer that.

His arm came slowly to his side, and he seemed in the shadows to become smaller, his thin-boned shoulders curling forward around his lizard years. He stared at me out of the shadows of his eye sockets, but he was Grandfather now, standing in his clothes with his pipe in his mouth. He shuffled forward, and his hand touched the open box of ax handles. He pulled one halfway out and looked at it as if he did not know what it was. Then he let it drop, turned, and shuffled down the aisle toward the elevator. I followed at a distance.

I stepped gingerly onto the elevator platform, afraid that the black man who controlled it would be caught off guard, and we would fall to the basement. Grandfather pulled the swaying rope that was tied to the black man, and greasy cables began to feed us downward, past shadowy floors, toward my father and the front door of Slate Hardware. I desired the front door of Slate Hardware. When I walked through it, I would not stop at the cannon plaque to count dents or search for copper BBs in the yard of the courthouse; I would just get into the Studebaker and leave with Father and go home to Mother—to my brand new home and Mother. Grandfather stooped in the corner of the elevator, the signal rope playing through his circled hand. I looked up through the dim mauve void of the shaft and saw that what had happened was like the secret I had. I had one secret. It was walking in on my big brother Graham and my cousin Debbie lying on top of each other on the bathroom floor. Now I had two. I would not tell anyone.

The wind played across my neck as the platform descended to my mother. I would crawl into bed with her and sleep in the crack between Father. I had done that once before when a bear lumbered up the steps in my dream, stood on his hind legs and switched on a light bulb, which danced and jiggled across his huge brown head, as he smiled and said softly, Come out Austen, we know you are there, and I hid behind hollow cardboard boxes and fainted awake. There were bears in this store, but they were all above and below the ground floor, except the one on the bullet display. The ground floor was just a normal place. Up here the bears awakened at nightfall. Maybe the black man fed them before he went home from work— or they fed themselves in the forest of hardware, padding quietly past thick timbers, breathing on the metal of stoves and engines. I stood in the center of the platform so they could not reach me as we passed downward, silently daring them to try when we neared the first floor. But I looked at Grandfather and saw that he had let go of the signal rope, turned toward me, and was shuffling across the moving platform, as the first floor came into view and then disappeared above, and we were swallowed in dark, my stomach tugging gently downward as he brushed by me—a shadow of burned tobacco. At his touch I half turned, losing my balance and grabbing the air so I wouldn't fall. Grandfather had left the controls, and I must not move my feet from the center of the platform. He was absorbed in the cold that breathed across me. He had gone off to finish what he was doing. He would call for me, and I would have to take off my clothes and walk through the basement to him. Bears would stop and wait. If I looked up into the gloom of the shaft, the black man would take me to him. I lost my balance again, and my arms jerked to keep my feet exactly where they stood. Balance regained, I hunched my head between my shoulders and methodically felt the blackness around me with fingers stiffened into nails. I protected a circle around me.

A match flared not far away, illuminating Grandfather's face and pipe. He lit the pipe, then switched on a light bulb that hung in front of his head, and his forehead was like white paper that you could see through. He stood in the pool of light, shuffling through a metal box on a long table. Then the light was switched out, and the glowing pipe was above me, speaking, "I got a present for you, boy. Hold out your hand."

Something small and cold was put in my palm.

"That's a bullet," he said. "Belle Starr was carrying it when they shot her."

"Yessir."

"Do you like that present, Austen?" There was a tone in his voice that I had never heard before. "Do you, boy?"

"Yessir."

"They took it off her dead body."

I did not know what he was talking about.

"It's worth money . . . I hope that little present, I hope it will occupy your mind." His voice seemed to be asking me for something.

I squeezed the bullet in my wet hand. "Yessir."

"My father gave it to me." For a second his hand touched my shoulder. And then the question was out of his voice. "Anyway, that's the best I can do. Don't lose it."